C000180275

# Ghosts of the Old Year

PARTHIAN BOOKS

# GHOSTS OF THE OLD YEAR

## New Welsh Short Fiction

PARTHIAN BOOKS

Parthian
The Old Surgery
Napier Street
Cardigan
SA43 1ED
www.parthianbooks.co.uk

First Published in 2003
©The Authors
All Rights Reserved
Ghosts of the Old Year 2003

ISBN 1-902638-27-1
Typeset in Galliard by NW

Printed and bound by Dinefwr Press, Llandybie

The publishers acknowledge the financial support of the Rhys
Davies Trust in the publication of this book.

The Rhys Davies Trust is a charity which has as its aim the
fostering of Welsh writing in English.

*A Human Condition*, the selected stories of Rhys Davies, is
published by Parthian.

Published with the assistance of

THE RHYS DAVIES TRUST

With support from the Parthian Collective

A cataloguing record for this book is available from the British
Library

Cover design & photography: Jo Mazelis
Edited by Jessica Mordsley

For Rhys, and his stories

## The Stories

# WOMAN RECUMBENT

## Stevie Davies

**Stevie Davies's** family came from Morriston but moved to Newton and later Mumbles. For thirteen years she worked as a university lecturer in Manchester. Stevie has published 23 books – fiction, biography, literary criticism and history – and is a Fellow of the Royal Society of Literature. Currently she is Royal Literary Fund Writing Fellow at the University of Wales Swansea. Her last novel, *The Element of Water*, won the Arts Council of Wales Book of the Year award for 2002.

After a day and a night of lying on bare tiles, shafts of cold penetrating her pelvis, hooping her chest, if human warmth ever came, it would strike like a grenade. Libby set rock-hard, puzzled at her rigidity when she inclined to move. Pain was glaciated, fear glazed. In the old days, the clemency of pneumonia would long ago have commuted her sentence: 'the old man's friend'. That friend had several times tapped lightly at her door, dithered and been turned away by the authorities.

Prone on the kitchen floor, she spasmodically caught (as an eye twitched open) the wink of house-keys hung high on a ring. Through the open door to the sitting room her glance angled the faint cream glow of a wall-mounted phone. Once, waking, she thought, *it is never wholly dark. All night round light wanes but never succeeds in failing.*

Otherwise how could the remote keys, the phone hanging as it seemed in space, remain discernible? Men had space-walked on umbilical ropes. They had floated out where there was no height or depth, neither up nor down. In this cold, and with a cracked hip or thigh, which she had heard snap doubly like distant twigs, the kinesis had failed that might power an effortful raising of head, torso, belly, from the tiles. At first there was a dimming, then suspense, now fractional intimation of renewal: on the point of extinction light rallied, to tip dull mist on to dusty surfaces. Her immediate world was bounded by the edge of a dingy mat, inches from her face. How frayed it was, rimmed with hairs like lashes, or

11

a centipede's legs, grease-clogged. For years her soles had worn themselves thriftily thin on this mat, a squalid object if you thought about it, but its proximity now brought a tinge of dark comfort, like some pet, mangy and disgraceful, but known.

She was numb to time. Chill glazed Libby's mind and the long pauses between pulse beats stretched away untenably until the heart beat (unexpected by now) came with a soft explosive startle of her whole body. There was no horror, none. Only the icy abstraction of waiting in death's antechamber, so near to this familiar mat, with pearls of light dewing the pane of the living room window (for the door was open, ready to walk through with a tray of tea). An idea distilled. *Pull down the drying up cloth, lay your head on that.* It dangled above her, and so did the idea, but though she urged herself to claw, hook, flip, drag it somehow down, she could perform this only in imagination: her body withheld assent. Such baffling impotence impelled Libby to try again and again, enacting her project solely on the mental plane, whilst her hands maintained metal-cold inertia and her head continued unpillowed. Her skull might have cracked open like an egg, and all her yolk slopped out, so concussively hard had she come down.

It dawned on Libby, hearing the sough of early commuting traffic on the Swansea road, that she must have spent her last or penultimate night on earth. They would all carry on threshing in and out of a city that had long been less of a memory than a rumour in her solitude; and she would be out of it. Well out of it. Yet some spasmodic instinct still thrust up towards warmth and life: the quickening sap of hope hurt mortally. Tresses of light wavered on the carpet and against the armchair in the living room, so comfy, so ordinary, holding the shape of Libby's light frame. The curtains remained apart like wide eyelids: there'd been no time to close them before being caught short by this whatever-it-was, this seizure. Or had she tripped on something? A ruck of mat? Had someone got in and assaulted her, how could you know? All around her consciousness the house was open to the light of day.

Nakedly open. Strange shame confounded Libby, lying here on the rust-red tiles, at the prospect of being found, her body putrefied perhaps, beyond recognition. How ghastly for them: she hoped it would not be Ceri, her young neighbour, great granddaughter of Libby's decades-dead childhood friend, also a Ceri. *I'm just popping in, Mrs Vaughan. Brought you some baked rice with a cinnamon skin, I know how you like it.*

They would blame Danny for not coming regularly to check on her. For always having excuses: *I've got work to go to, a living to make, I can't be round there all the time, it's just not on, sorry.* Poppers-in twisted the knife in Danny's sullen back. *Ah*, they cooed, in unsubtle rebuke, *she's such a spry soul, isn't it, you must be proud to have such an alert, intelligent mam, 94 years of age, and all her wits about her!*

And he made that face, that (to Elizabeth) highly legible face which had first appeared when he went away to school, a stricken guilty-angry scowl, bending his grey head like a schoolboy and mumbling. He had been the unintended child of her age, his debilitating presence in her belly mistaken for the onset of menopause until he could no longer be ignored as a human burden.

Danny wouldn't come. Why should he? She did not blame him. Not a whit. She should beg his pardon for knocking him down.

Had she indeed knocked him down? On her motor bike? In the war she had sped through bombed-out Swansea bearing letters as a courier but could not recall knocking anyone down, let alone her one son. But he had come a cropper: of that there was no doubt. It was a conundrum and she let it go. Light washed on the green settee; it must be breezy out there. When you peed yourself lying here, for a moment the sensation was warm and comforting, then colder than before. Danny had been a bed-wetter: she had smacked, they endorsed violence to children in those days. And you, criminally, obeyed. A rapture of black impatience quivered through her: why couldn't it be over, the

13

punishment? Why be put on this earth, to rot like this, at tedious length? To suffer interminable resurrections. It is unnecessary, she thought. It contributes and amounts to nothing whatever. It is uneconomic.

Uncle Evan with his healthy brutality, his sense of timing, had given equal weight to economy and mercy. With one clean wring of the neck Evan would slaughter chickens. Shot the tired and gallant mare through the temple. Libby had looked Jenny-Jill in the eye before uncle despatched her. Trustfully she'd clopped along to her death between uncle and niece, the tumour in her belly pendant as though she were in foal. Elizabeth, gazing into the patience of Jenny-Jill's eye, had fingered her velvety muzzle in awed valediction, the tapering bone so solidly defined; rushed away into the farmhouse at uncle's bidding and left Jenny-Jill to his canny mercy.

*Crack* went the pistol-shot. And your hip which was friable as a dead twig, porous, its vital juices and calcium leeched, cracked one evening, once, twice. No one came to offer the clemency of a bullet, a shot in the arm, nor had you means to make an honourable, a Roman, end of it. The long freeze perpetuated itself. Libby shut her eyes, to seal out the fringe on the mat, dust-puffs and decaying crumbs, the wanton bloom of light on the couch through the door. Everything drifted down in a fine silt, the leavings, skin-flakes, coffee-particles, dust powdering surfaces like a pall of ash.

In this extremity appeared the most minor of miracles. A creaturely presence. The ant had scurried from somewhere into Elizabeth's field of vision, where it now paused. Her jaw and cheek burned with the atrocity of cold as if her face were one giant toothache, while her eyes took in the visitation. It had roamed far from its nest: perhaps the community sent out scouts, to reconnoitre territory. And doubtless the ant, with its superior senses, intuited as foreign the presence of the mountain-range of skeletal flesh that was Elizabeth, the foothills of her skirts, and waited irresolute, so near to her milky-blue eyes. She was herself terrain now.

Libby pondered the ant. The habit of intelligence was tenacious. She felt bound to take the ant into consideration. It was a life after all. A creature at eye-level. Nothing to do with her, and what a relief. Inhabiting its own proximate world. You put down poison for the colony. It didn't work, in her experience. A puddle of bleach sometimes did the trick. A cluster of brethren drowned, alerting the corporate mind. Then they'd all decamp. Disappear from the cracks in the tiled sill which was the entrance to their nether kingdom, pouring out to forage, pouring in with supplies, only to reappear on the counter by the bread bin. She didn't much mind them. But she had never before been glad of one. She kept her eye on the ant, until it no longer seemed as miniscule, but a companionate presence which she tacitly saluted.

And there beside it, one human hair. White, curved, single. How come she had not seen it before? It lay in an arc, curving toward the mat with its eyelash-fringe. One of her own hairs, for certain; yet it seemed alien, not pertaining to her as she essentially was, despite the fact that she had been grey for decades. Or rather, pure white, and sparse, so that the scalp showed through a fluffy cloud. But that this should be *her* hair, detritus of *her* head, and not her mother's or grandmother's, puzzled Libby, as if a system had slipped.

Detached, the hair lay there, next to the ant, which appeared to have moved. Presumably as she'd pushed her hair back from her forehead yesterday or the day before, this individual had detached, hanging by a follicle to her jumper, then slipped away into these reaches she had never imagined. Indeed, why should she? What would be the utility? The schoolmistressy riposte rapped out in her head like a ruler on a desk (what attitudinising piffle it had all been, though, the geography and Scripture, the gold stars and the black marks, considering the finality of this perspective, getting down to it, level with this ant, that hair). Perhaps now, soon, she could be quit, make her quietus.

\*

A face youthful at the window, craning. Consternation seizing the face. Not Daniel, because of course Daniel was grizzled now, on the cusp of middle-age. The young face was jabbering but she failed to make out the words. His eyebrows worked, his hands flapped. Her heart's sap surged, with painful warmth. If she could have moved, Elizabeth would have shooed Jason the Milk away. Now it was all up, they would resuscitate her. Having got so far, the deathly cold having seized her feet and calves in such a vice that she could no longer feel them at all, certain bones having snapped, her mind having pitched down this cliff, they would abort her journey. They would importune her, *You must rise again, so that you can die again.* Like all acts of public benevolence, this alienation of her rights would be reinforced by violence.

'It's all right, Mrs Vaughan, my love, don't you be scared, darling, I'm coming through the window. Only way, see.'

A fountain of glass smithereened; the morning imploded; but its shock was unregistered until the warm male hand cupped her head, lifting it from the tiles on to her sheepskin. Then she was shaken with grief at the sight of Jason's tears as he stammered into his mobile phone, rushed for a blanket, covered her and chafed her hands with their great knots of vein, so that warmth prickled into her slow-sliding blood.

'Don't you worry now, darling, ambulance is on its way. Thank goodness it's one of your milk days.'

A slight, fair-skinned boy, crew-cut, a ring in one earlobe. Observing the gleaming lobe in the sun-slant, Libby despaired. You ran the egg and spoon race, ran it for safety not for speed, loping on your long legs, plaits bouncing on your shoulder-blades, balancing the egg carefully: and though you came in last and all the other lasses had vanished, vanished long ago (because you excelled in caution and stamina, longevity was in your maternal genes, frugality and a spartan diet in your traditions, a brainy, resourceful, bookish girl) - despite all this, you had the tape in sight. And now just within reach, you dropped your egg.

'What was that, Mrs Vaughan, lovely?' The earring bent

to her mouth.

    'Humpty.'

    'Don't you worry now, be here any minute.'

    He treated her like a child. Thought she'd gone off her rocker, when in point off fact she had never known such luminous clarity. For (it burst upon her now, with Jason's hand cradling both hers) she never should have had a child. Even the one. Too bony, too hawkish, cerebral, opinionated. She had done wrong by Daniel from the first. Reading Sophocles - Sophocles! - while she fed her baby in the night. *Not to be born is best.* Oh yes, a very nice lullaby when you are hesitantly sucking your rubber teat, a lovely welcome to this world. Closing her ears when he cried. Banishing him to the Siberia of school at the earliest opportunity.

    Life means life. When the judge imposed his sentence, he stipulated, *in this woman's case, life must mean life.*

    She was raised on the stretcher by men in yellow coats, wheeled out into the mouth of the morning. Her own lips gaped apart and she lapsed asleep.

*

The intuition reared that Danny had died: that he had lain prone on a cold floor with people kicking him, coiled foetally to hug his head. She'd sent him into this zone of violence, driven him out. For every time he had to go away, Danny had wrung his hands at the station, at which she betrayed him, saying, *You'll be all right, Daniel. Soon as you get there.* And he had begged, every time, *But.* She spoke over his *but.* They both did. She and Huw, who'd crammed Dan's blazer pockets with sweets till they bulged, not meeting those brimming eyes. She had driven him off, out, away, go, shoo. The train pulled in with roars, hisses, shocks of smoke and the stink of sulphur. Her fingertips poked into the boy's tender back as he mounted the steep steps. Up he must go, up; stand tall, like the other boys. She waited, desperate for the whistle to blow. And he said *But mam please.* Now he had fallen. Under the train? She wanted to ask the man in the yellow coat but a plastic beak over her mouth and nose, with oxygen flowing

17

through it, impeded speech. No, she grasped the recognition, the reassurance, as it flashed through her brain, it was not Danny who had fallen, thank God, but herself who had been lying on the kitchen floor with the cold kicking up into her slack belly, her pouched cheek.

*

'Come to see your mam? We were becoming quite concerned, Mr Vaughan, we couldn't get hold of you. She'll be so relieved to see you, thinks you've had an accident. Ah, a lovely lady, your mam. Don't worry, she's doing just great.'

His shoulders sagged. His eloquent eyebrows drooped.

*Yes*, Elizabeth seemed to hear her son say. *I sometimes think she's immortal.*

'Well, of course, she took a nasty fall. But she came through the operation lovely.'

'Good.'

'Be a relief to you, I know. Mrs Vaughan, here's your son to see his mam. Doesn't say much at present, there's always an element of trauma.'

'Yes, I know.'

'Danny. You needn't have come, I'm quite all right, I didn't want you to fall, you know that. But I should have kept you safe. You should have had an alarm, one of those gadgets with a bleep, it's connected to a carer, you didn't even have a phone, did you, and if you had, how could you have reached, darling, being such a little boy for your age? Actually of course we didn't have a phone either in those days, and if we had, would I have answered? They say my hearing's acute, but is it? I sometimes think I'm congenitally stone-deaf. I was preoccupied, it was my books, you see, but what excuse is that? I don't ask your forgiveness, no, for letting you fall under the train, it was sheer negligence, I can see that now, and you never got over it, never, I can see that too just from the way your shoulders hunch and you duck your head to one side as if someone were going to cuff you. You should have had home helps, you should have had more than just someone popping in to check up on you and breezing out and then I'm convinced you would *not* have fallen.'

She spoke her mind with her usual crackling asperity. Daniel was leaning forward and appeared to be listening intently. His breath came fast and shallow as his hand crept toward hers across the starched linen.

*But mam*, he said, and couldn't go on.

# THE GHOSTS OF THE OLD YEAR

## Jo Mazelis

**Jo Mazelis** was born in Swansea. Her work has appeared widely in magazines, anthologies and has also been broadcast on Radio 4. She is the only writer to have received the Rhys Davies Award three times. In addition to her writing she works as a designer and photographer. Her first collection of stories *Diving Girls* was published in 2002. She has lived and worked in London and Aberystwyth.

She has a Welsh daughter and an American husband. She lives on a hill in Swansea and has a very small view of the sea.

I won't admit to loneliness. That is too much of a sign of weakness, a sign of defeat. I don't want pity, but I don't want this empty night pressing down on me.

The baby is asleep now and that leaves her absence; her silence in the room like a great hole. Remember the story of Jesus in the Garden. It was his last night of freedom, and the others, his friends fell asleep. He couldn't sleep knowing what he knew but they slept. I wonder what they dreamed that night, those ghosts of long ago.

My baby sleeps. She has no ghosts. She laughs at the pictures I have painted of my ghost. My ghost is a smiling woman. I keep the paintings hidden. They are my secret. They are all the same, these pictures. There was just one photograph to paint from. I found it in his wallet.

There, you see how I am; sly and jealous and full of rage. I can't help it, though. She has done this to me. So now I must work some evil on her. And so I paint her. I like to use wrong colours, to paint like Matisse, Rouault, Dufy, Derain. They called them the wild beasts and that suits me. That is how I feel. I give my ghost all her prettiness. I never take the baby plumpness from her cheeks, nor the brightness from her eyes nor do anything to mar her two perfect dimples. She must look as she looks in the photograph; beautiful, desirable, sweet. All I do is give her green skin or red eyes or black lips.

These are probably my best paintings. But no one will see

them. I'll make sure of that. I keep the pictures in my wardrobe. Her face is pressed against the rough wood in the darkness and that way I am safe. That way she is in my power. I can take the memories in and out of the cupboard at will, give myself little doses of pain like medicine and try to forget.

I remember the time before as a golden age. I was happy. It's true that often he disappeared for hours, days, weeks even but I would sit with the baby happily suckling at my breast and feel content. Four months went by like that and I looked forward to Christmas like I hadn't for a long time. Since I was a child I suppose, when I was filled with all the longing for carol singing and chocolate and tangerines and the thrill of waking up on Christmas morning to find at my feet the heavy weight of one of my father's old socks filled to brimming with presents.

Now for the first time I was a mother and I could live it all over again for my child. I would make each Christmas a magic time with soft fairy lights and angels everywhere and the smell of pine. The dream was like a Christmas bauble, all shiny glass, brightly coloured, hollow, fragile.

He didn't come back. I waited up all Christmas Eve, telling myself that he was out there somewhere searching for a taxi, walking through the gone to bed streets of Swansea. What if there had been an accident and he lay dying? I saw myself, a brave and weeping widow with a baby in my arms at his graveside. I pushed the idea away and thought he must be drunk and how he'd turn up the next day, sorry and sweet, his arms filled with mistletoe and presents and love.

Christmas day passed like any other, except that the streets were empty, the shops and cafés closed and when I went out for a walk and looked at other people I saw in them perfect happiness. Their smiles and laughter loomed large and rosy, and I passed like a wraith away from them, a little match girl in my misery. I kept my eyes on the pavement ahead with my eyes following the grey slanting shadow-shape of a lone woman pushing a pram.

He was with her, of course. She had wiped me from his

mind with one look and made him forget his daughter with her light dancing laughter. I blame her for everything. I blame her for her blue eyes and slow smile. I blame her for her soft breasts and the taut skin of her belly. I see the facade of her nineteen-year-old face and underneath it I sense only wickedness and cruelty.

I read the baby a fairy tale in which beauty is good and age and ugliness bad, and I curse the princess who could not sleep because of a pea beneath her mountain of mattresses and I curse all the princes who believe that she is the only true good woman in the world.

So I paint the nameless ghost in red and green and purple. Yellow eyes and vermilion teeth, black tongue and emerald skin. I paint her as the snow queen all wintry white and icy, with kisses that will freeze his heart and make him forget his little Gerda.

It was New Year's Eve when I found his jacket and hugged it to me wanting him, missing him, still fearful of the overturned car that may have killed him, the drink that made him sleep in the ditch until he died half frozen. I lay down on the bed and held it like I wanted to hold him and my hand found his wallet and I took it out and opened it. There inside was the photograph.

I handled the snapshot like a precious relic or a thing cursed. I set it on the table and sat on the other side of the room. Occasionally I'd get up and go and look at it again.

It was only a photograph. Only a smiling woman on a summer's day with a ribbon in her hair. Yet she became summer itself, and turned me into winter.

As the day wore on I began to avoid the table, walking in gradually wider circles around it, averting my eyes from the grinning succubus I had set free. I could not concentrate on anything except the photograph. I tried to read while the baby took her midday nap, but the words on the page were a useless jumble of ill-expressed sentiment that had no meaning. The smile of the succubus filled the room and stopped the clocks and pressed against my chest until I gasped for air.

It began to grow dark at two o'clock, I was not sure

which one of us had pulled the sky down like a vast grey blanket heavy with snow, but the day was gone, the sun lost forever.

I wondered what I should do to exorcise this ghost. I could stub my cigarette out on her face, burn the photograph, tear it up, obliterate the smile, the ribbon in her hair, the summer dress. Slowly gouge out the blue eyes, cut the hair from her scalp, scratch through her with a pen, furiously criss-crossing her image until she was all gone, but she wouldn't be gone, she would merely become more elusive. To destroy her I had to know her. That was the secret.

The baby woke then and I opened my blouse and guided her mouth to my nipple and she sucked and patted the full milky flesh of my breast with her little hand and sighed her satisfied sighs. In the stillness my hurt took the shape of anger, my fear became revenge and I wondered if my raging thoughts would turn the milk sour and poison the child in my arms.

The night slipped away into sleep and my dreams were the dreams of the haunted. In the nightmare I went into the bedroom, though for what reason I cannot tell, and the ghost was there curled in his arms. That same smile from the photograph fixed on her lips for eternity. I found my hand suddenly tightening around a knife and I raised it high ready to strike, but as I watched she seemed to shrink and fade away until it was only the baby that slept against his warmth. I stopped my hand and as I did my daughter opened her eyes and seeing me began to cry and I awoke to the black confusion of night and the real sobbing of my child.

The next day I knew what I must do. I stretched and sized a canvas, taking more care with its taut surface that I had ever done before. Its whiteness seemed to draw me in, speaking of a peace and purity I had never before noticed. I was not afraid as I usually am, to make the first mark. It was not going to be a beautiful painting, one to hang in a gallery and sell, but one that would live with me, be right or wrong with me, and would perhaps eventually be destroyed by me.

The first painting took nearly two months to complete, I

worked at it every chance I got. January passed like one long night. I don't remember seeing daylight but somehow the baby grew and I fed her and washed her and loved her. By mid February I was on my second canvas, I knew the woman's face well by then, so that the merest flick of my brush could indicate an eye, and it was her eye.

Now it is January again and there are thirteen paintings, each one more loose and vibrant than the last. They are my best work. They are as beautiful as the cobwebs on Miss Haversham's wedding cake and as flawless as the nails in Marley's coffin. The thirteenth will be the last. It is the perfect number. It is the number of Judas as he reaches forward in the garden to betray the man who hasn't slept.

Once I am certain that my daughter is sound asleep, I clear away her playthings, the beloved debris of the day, and bring out all the pictures. I prop them up around the room; against the table, the playpen, the high chair, the settee, and I sit cross-legged on the rug with them circling me. I am a stone in a ring of bright flowers, blanched of colour, empty of feeling.

I close my eyes. Open them again. This is my garden, these my paints, my colours, my light. I am not a stone, impassive, without art. I am a gardener, a god, and tomorrow is a new morning.

# WATERSHED

## Rhodri Clark

**Rhodri Clark** was born and brought up in the Rhymney Valley and now lives in Conwy. After studying music in Manchester, he began a career in journalism, working for *The Western Mail* and various magazines. Writing fiction is a hobby for him (although some might say that's what he does in his day job).

# Dear Mrs X,

Dear Mrs X! It's the New Year and I've resolved to communicate more effectively, so here I am writing to you without even knowing your new surname.

I should congratulate you on tying the knot, but doing that would break my resolution to communicate fully and frankly from now on. I'm not jealous, you must understand, just saddened by the legacy of poor communication.

We were both happy until our eyes first met, weren't we? Ignorance is the best chaperone for happiness; when we escaped its clutches we saw greener pastures in the distance, where happiness lay at the foot of a rainbow. Since humans can't erase experiences, neither of us will ever return to our former state of absolute happiness. We can try to be relatively happy, to be as content as possible, just as we might wish to recreate the original line of a broken nose while knowing the nose will never overcome its history. Meanwhile, our ignorance can only sulk in the background, queueing with the long-term unemployed.

Why do we marry so young in my valley? Out of boredom, I suppose. There's nothing else to do when you live in a stagnant ditch. We had our ambitions too, just like you. Mainly the ambition to get the hell out of the place, but in our valley the population's batteries were too flat for aspirations to assume a material worth. It's all down to vitamin deficiency, no doubt.

Deficiency arising from severe lack of sunshine.

I was so desperate to see the sun that I went for a walk on Tuesday, up to the ridge where I could pry into your valley's daily routine like a nosy neighbour peering from a darkened room. Winter in our valley can't be much different from winter in Lapland. The sun lacks the strength, or the motivation, to reach over the mountains and fondle our houses. For us a sunny day is a cold day, when the earth's heat escapes through the troposphere and our pallid faces are lit by the reflection of a clear sky. On such occasions we gaze upwards and start to dream, because there is no limit to our vision.

Then we'll have weeks of drizzle to turn our dreams into a soggy mush on the pavements. A grey lid is bolted down to the mountaintops, arching from the forest of everblack trees on one slope to the everblack trees on the other. You can have no idea what it's like to eke out an entire life in a prime habitat of woodlice and moss; when I looked down into your valley on Tuesday I saw the sunlight splashing over the houses. I imagined you growing up there, your cheeks and the backs of your legs reddened by the daily sun. I pretended to pick out your childhood home among the proud terraces. Three miles away from my house you were, by my estimation. Three miles, that's all.

I can't wheel out the cliché that we were made for each other in a letter like this, but you know as well as I what happened that night we first saw each other in London. Within a week we had spent those three or four frantic hours together. We squeezed a supply of sexual energy meant for a lifetime into one afternoon, in a cheap hotel in that huge impersonal city where secrets can last forever. We both realised that we were two jigsaw pieces made to slot together. Sadly, we can also make a fraudulent but passable fit with other pieces, an ostrich solution that ensures the big picture of contentment is never completed.

So, there we were, spending our formative years three miles apart but never meeting until we'd travelled too far. I blame my father. Of course I blame my father. That's what parents are for. To start with they're helpful - stopping you eating dog shit or running under buses - but as you develop their help grows harmful. When I first became aware that a parallel world existed outside our gully, my dad frowned and said, "You don't want to go there, my boy. It's bad as Sodom and Gomorrah over there."

He was trying to be helpful, but look what that did to me – to us!

"Full of criminals it is, stealing each other's property, fighting, drinking and spitting. And there's bad language, drugs … the lot. They don't just live in sin there, they eat and drink in sin. And they sleep and sweat and fart in sin."

"Are they English, dad?"

"Might as well be," he muttered.

The charge was leaking from my batteries already. If only he'd been less helpful I would have been over to your valley a few years later. There's no way we would have missed each other.

Some time afterwards I learned that my dad had never been to your valley himself. He was basing his judgement on hearsay, crime reports in the papers and the innate fear of everyone in our village of having the truth tortured into them.

If only communications had been better between our valleys! (There's no road between them, just a forest path that becomes a stony farm track and passes through dozens of gates before becoming metalled and worthy of flowing into the road system on your side.) Then my dad might have known what kind of people lived in your Sodom and Gomorrah and I, in due course, would not have lived in ignorance of those silky legs of yours carrying those eyes, those breasts, that breath, that laughter around the valley.

Why did we run away from each other after that afternoon of love? Remorse on your part, I should think. You were a few weeks away from getting hitched to an Englishman with an excellently dull career and there you were in that hotel going all the way, and beyond, with a married man from "back home", from "The Welsh Valleys", as any outsider would see it. As for me:

I fled, from you and my feelings, in anger. I was furious with my valley, that puddle of black water where I was destined to pass my life swimming in tight circles. I've crawled out and seen the rest of the world now – long after marrying someone from my own gene pool and bringing two little girls into the same environment of rotting wood and rotten self-esteem.

The other day – Tuesday, it was – I thought of you on your honeymoon in Mauritius. I imagined you were sitting in the shade of coconut palms, to escape the attentions of a zealous sun. I was grabbed by a desire to see sunshine myself. Like a liana in a jungle, I had to climb through the forest canopy. But in my forest there are no monkeys, macaws or spiders. The sole animal life is the bacteria turning this year's needles into food for next year's desultory growth, the same nutrients locked into an incestuous cycle to help the trees lock us into our home villages. There's no light on the forest floor, so nothing has the urge to grow there.

In the autumn the Japanese larches turn a golden colour, but no-one notices because gold is spectacular only in the presence of bright light. The trees, wiry, loyal and fatigued, stand shoulder-to-shoulder along the hillsides like the advance guard for an invasion by Japanese industrialists. The lower branches are grey and skeletal. Twigs snap underfoot like warning shots from pathetic, neglected pistols. As you climb through the forest the odd malnourished tree trunk croaks through the silence as it struggles to stay upright. Is this army dead or simply sleeping on its feet?

On gaining the ridgetop, the boundary of that sloping parade ground, I had to half-close my eyes against the glare of the sunsplash. I hadn't seen such bright light since summer, and then only for brief spells. At the same time my nostrils were assailed with the smells of gorse and sheep and breezes, the smells of vigorous life, of ambition borne of photosynthesis. As I walked on over the springy, joyous turf I heard the squeaking of skylarks as they flitted low over the ground. Then, as your valley came into view, I spotted a pair of large birds – peregrines, perhaps – wheeling. I must have spent a full hour leaning on a five-bar gate, feeling the wind buffeting at my back like a playful lion cub demanding attention. I was mesmerised by the sight of a valley where the greenery gushed down to the houses and trickled on even farther, over playing fields and parks, and where ancient stone farmhouses clung for position beside the vast trapezia of landscaped spoil-heaps – the green apple of some planning official's eye. Disembodied notes from Match of the Day drifted up from a squawking ice-cream van among the terraces. I watched the cars and lorries zipping along the trunk road, cross-pollinating your village and the wider world. Beneath my feet sprawled a retail park of shoebox shapes. I picked out a DIY store where sunlight flashed off the cars as they scurried in and out of the car park, fuelled by their drivers' perpetuating enthusiasm for order, repair and improvement.

I turned away from this diorama and bent my shoulders into the wind. Back on the ridgetop, I stood like a Celtic hero – in neither valley and in both at the same time – and savoured my ambivalence a while. It was still a sunny day in your valley. The streetlights had been switched on in my valley, where dozens of house windows showed as yellow pinpricks. I was in night and day simultaneously, and yet in neither night nor day.

In one direction, I could see the sun tempting me to start a new and bigamous life by pretending I belonged in an alien town. If English pensioners can settle in Malaga and Majorca, then I could transplant myself to Llanfair El Dorado, ostensibly for the benefit of my chest, my heart and my joints.

I looked over my other shoulder. Nothing moved in the gloom. I peered down into a starry sky where I could name every constellation: Agatha Street, Thomas Street, Ebenezer Row, Forge Street, the Labour Club car park.

I began to walk briskly towards them. The cosmopolitan wind, which has already passed many countries yet always heads for the next one, showed its disappointment. It urged me to turn back and descend into your valley but 'hiraeth', the congenital curse on every Welsh heart, was pulling me forwards, into my own square mile where the villages wander lazily into one another without definition, like the lines of the local family trees, and where everyone breathes the same air over and over again. I felt a thirst for a drink at the Royal Oak with my mates Danny and Gar and John, a thirst for the familiarity in which I must gradually rebuild happiness and contentment without you.

Goodbye, my love.

PS: Of course, I can't send this letter. In truth it's addressed to me, not you.

# TEN QUID FOR A BUSTED CASIO

## Brian George

**Brian George** was born in Rhondda, but now lives in Pontypool. He has worked as a teacher, lecturer and now schools adviser. His stories and poems have been published in a number of Welsh and English magazines, his articles and submissions on contemporary French theatre and popular music have been included in a variety of academic publications and he is currently putting together a collection of stories for publication.

Hello. I'm Judith Edwards, wife of Jeff and devoted mother to Rachel and Ceri. Jeff and I have had a long, fulfilling marriage, blessed with two wonderful children. Bright, beautiful, successful, well-adjusted girls on the threshold of womanhood. A credit to our skills and commitment as parents. As the years pass Jeff and I are mellowing into contented maturity. The foundations of our happy partnership were laid a long time ago, and stem from our early rejection of the romantic delusions most couples fill their heads with. Even on our wedding day. There we were, me and Jeff, ready to face the world. Together forever, but not heads in the clouds. No, we were feet on the ground, fortified by three years of living together, most of it in the kind of places you'd think twice about inflicting on a dog you cared about. Yes, me and Jeff. Together. Forever. Togetherforever.

OK, I know, that was all bullshit. Let's start again. My name's Judith Edwards. I have a husband, Jeff, and two sullen daughters. Jeff and I don't talk much. Right now, I'm a long way from home, sitting at a wonky formica-topped table, listening to the stranger opposite talking. We've been thrown together by chance in a spartan terraced house. In the darkening back kitchen he talks, I listen. He listens, I talk. As we talk I become aware of myself, for the first time in years, as a woman with something to say, being listened to by a man who looks me straight in the eye and smiles, quite simply, at what he sees there.

The man's name is Peter Watkins. He's quite small, about

five foot nine, and thin as a whippet. The first thing you notice is his fingers, which are surprisingly long and graceful. I know a little about him. He's ten years younger than me, in his late thirties, and lives alone with his teenage daughter. He somehow manages to make a living crafting handmade guitars, and his skill is semi-legendary in this valley. I think I would like to see him at work and to listen to him explain each stage of the process. He smiles as he looks at me, but it's a smile edged with sorrow and resignation. I want to find out his secrets, unravel the past that's eating him up. I need to try out his touch.

We talk endlessly. There are points we have to discuss, possessions whose fate it is our sad duty to decide. We methodically tackle the difficult tasks we are charged with, skirting round the thing that is taking shape between us. I decide he likes me. I know I am knocked for six by him. I also sense that this fascination will continue over weeks, months, growing into a sad obsession, long after the chance circumstances which brought us together have disappeared and we are separated by hundreds of miles. I will suffer all the usual pangs of uncertainty and unrequited love. I can already perceive many of the details shaping up. The letters I will write and consign to the bin. The bouts of incessant, uncontrolled weeping. The heroic, but ultimately futile, efforts we will make to ensure love triumphs against impossible odds. This will truly be a story to rend hearts, a doomed, impossible affair to set alongside the great tragic stories of couples fated never to live out their love. Me Heloise, Peter Abelard.

OK, I'm losing it again. Let's try one more time. My name's Judith Edwards, but you can call me Scheherazade if you like. We're all at it, telling stories every minute of the day. To ourselves, to each other. Trying to understand, trying to deceive. Me, I tell stories to stave off the inevitable, to slow time down. And right now, I'm clinging to the company of a fragile beauty which crept up on me like a cat in the night when I was least expecting it, rubbed against my neck and could jump down and skedaddle any minute.

These stories I'm telling you, of course, they're just banal slices of heartache. Chapters in the decline of a menopausal woman. After all, I'm plain Judith Edwards, a person of little consequence, compensating for a life of mediocrity by weaving elaborate fantasies to ward off the truth. The truth? Now there's a tough nut to crack. And where does it lie?

Anyway, now it's my turn to listen as Peter tells a story. A story with an amazing central character, a man I thought I knew but seemingly didn't. A man of warmth, courage, principles, vision and considerable intellect. A heroic figure, respected by many, even his enemies, and revered by young firebrands all over this valley. A man who sacrificed his chances of happiness, comfort, love, family, career, all in the service of an ideal which became increasingly unfashionable as the years passed. My brother. Like I said, Peter is a good talker. I'm absorbed by his story, memorising the details for possible later use. It's a story which moves me deeply. A true story?

My brother Les died three days ago. Peter Watkins knew him better than anyone. That's why he's sitting face to face with me, talking earnestly, while between us on the formica sits a battered old trunk. When we opened it, the trunk was crammed to bursting with Les's junk, the accumulated debris of his life. Mostly papers, pamphlets, leaflets, books. We've binned most of it, but Peter occasionally sets aside items he deems to be of significance. As he draws to the end of his narrative about Les, he picks a crumpled A5 sheet of photocopied paper from the trunk, stares at it for a moment, smoothes it out, places it to one side. He carries on talking about the funeral arrangements.

'Hang on a minute,' I chime in. 'What's so special about that bit of paper? Surely that's one for the bin?'

Peter looks at me, picks up the paper and hands it over. It's a faded photocopy of an old ten pound note, the black line bisecting the queen's head testifying to the poor quality of the machine that produced it God knows how long ago. It takes me a moment to notice that the words 'ten pounds' have been scratched out and 'thirty pieces of silver' scrawled in their place. I stare back at Peter, my bewilderment and incredulity transparent. 'So...?' my eyes scream at him.

'It's a long story,' he begins. 'Do you want to brew some tea first?' I don't, impatient to hear him talk some more.

'August 1st, 1984.' He's into his stride instantly. 'The Official Receiver was coming to sequester the funds of the South Wales miners. Demonstration in Ponty. Les and I were there, with thousands of others outside the union office on Sardis Road. Singing, chanting, marching, banners...' He's getting carried away, turning poetic. 'A sea of colour, life.' He reins in the metaphor, adjusts his tone. 'Somebody inside the office threw a few dozen of these' - he gestures at the photocopy - 'out of the window. People went mad, fighting over them as they fluttered down. Like everyone thought they'd be some kind of memento, medal even, of a historic day. Symbol of a day of struggle, maybe the start of a revolution. Token of defiance of the whole capitalist system. Like the miners were saying, here's our money, take it, you bastards. See if we care.'

He stops again, glances at his watch. Strokes his bottom lip, bites the top one. 'Of course, it didn't turn out like that. Stories never finish the way you expect.' Here Peter blinks hard several times. I realise he's got the beginnings of a few wrinkles at the corner of his left eye. 'We had this young friend at the time, Jonathan, a real nutter, the kind who'd literally throw himself at the wagons as they crossed the picket lines. Well, a couple of months after the miners' strike was over he led a walkout in this pathetic little knicker and nightie factory he'd got himself a job in. Management provocation, cutting the lunch break by ten minutes. Hopeless case, we all knew Jonathan was on a hiding to nothing. Les advised him against it, told him he should negotiate a compromise deal. Jonathan wouldn't listen, of course, got himself sacked with half a dozen of the others who fell for it. A few days later he sent this' - Peter jerks a forefinger at the photocopy - 'to Les.'

Peter stops, stares at a spot on the wall behind me. 'Les shrugged it off, pretended he didn't care, trotted out the usual stuff about people losing their bearings in new and unfamiliar circumstances.' Peter shakes his head, takes another look at his watch. I should point out that this act of looking at his watch is a bit more than a casual sideways glance. His watch is a cheap, basic Casio digital with a broken black strap. He keeps it in his right jeans pocket and has to fish it out whenever he wants to check the time. He lingers over this action as though unsure how - or whether - to finish the story. There's a slight catch in his voice when he goes on.

'Jonathan decided to take matters into his own hands. Threw a brick through the MD's car as he drove through the picket line one morning, got himself arrested. Not a good time to mark yourself down to the magistrates as a vindictive militant. Even the Echo said six months was a bit harsh for a first offence, but that didn't help Jonathan much.' Another pause, this time slowly fingering the rim of the Casio. 'Anyway, most people said it was the screw they felt sorry for, the luckless bastard who found him hanging in his cell one morning a few weeks later. Bit of a hue and cry for a while, but that soon died down. I doubt if many people remember it now. Another story we've airbrushed out of our collective memory... One thing's for sure, though, that was the end for Les. Oh, he tried to carry on, pretend it was business as usual, but it was just a case of going through the motions after that.'

'Christ,' I say, genuinely shocked. 'I had no idea...' Peter nods, still staring into the middle distance, fishes out the Casio again. 'I'd better be getting back. Chloe will be wondering where I am. Can you manage a couple of hours after the funeral tomorrow? That should be enough to sort it all out.' We exchange polite goodbyes.

It's years since I've slept in this house, and I have a restless night, punctuated by fragmented dreams in which Peter and I meet up in crowded places of life and laughter. I arrive over and over again at airports, railway stations, bars, restaurants, catch sight of his face across distances packed with people, fight my way through, desperate to touch and embrace him, never managing to reach him before the dream breaks, the scene shifts. I wake in a panic, go downstairs, try obsessively to recall the details of his face, find myself hugging the curtains in the front room, talking aloud of my undying love. I stagger out into the back garden, neglected and overgrown, but with a single rose bush inexplicably not only still standing, but with one perfect red flower on it. It's a gorgeous crimson, with petals folded so intricately it seems artificial. I breathe in its impossibly sweet aroma, rub it against my face, then destroy the beauty, biting petals, swallowing mush, sobbing the whole while. I go back to bed, drift in and out of sleep.

It's late when I eventually get up. I don't spare a thought for Les as I get ready for the funeral. I'm like a fifteen year old, completely fixated on this guy I've only just met and whom I'll never see again after today. I know, I know. This thing we misname love is one of the main instruments for keeping women in their place. Turns us into helpless lumps of jelly, reduces us to half the people we could be. I know it's just a series of chemical reactions, assorted cocktails of dopamine, oxytocin and God knows what else going apeshit for a few days, weeks, months. Driving us crazy, fooling us into telling ourselves the tallest of tall stories. Stories we believe, poor suckers that we are.

I also know this thing is making me feel like a god, like a queen. I'm lord of creation and pathetic blob. Both at the same time. Sort that one out if you can.

The funeral itself is one of those rush jobs in the crem. Whip you in and out at top speed, maximise throughput. But Peter manages to work in a little speech, expanding the eulogy of Les that I heard him give yesterday. This time he tells it with a passion that takes not only me, but the rest of the sparse congregation, by storm. Despite my doubts about the story's veracity, I give myself up totally to Peter's gift for the telling. Somewhere deep, I deliquesce.

I'm catatonic through the little buffet at the sports centre after the funeral. I daresay some of the others mistake my vacant stares for numbed grief. *Look at her, poor thing. First her parents within six months of each other three years ago, now her only brother. Still, she's got that smashing husband to take care of her back in Manchester. Wonder where he is, by the way? Thought he'd have been here to lend some support...*

But before long here we are, back where we started. Sitting at a cheap table in my brother's house, the house I grew up in. Peter and I have finished sifting through the last of Les's belongings. He's going to see to the disposal of the rubbish, and to find a suitable home for the stuff he's decided is worth saving. He says there's a specialist library in London that will probably be glad to have it.

On the formica top the photocopied ten pound note sits in isolation. Peter is silent, obviously waiting for me to say something. For a moment I feel paralysed, then something clicks into place. 'Give me your watch,' I say. My voice, clear and self-assured, takes Peter aback. 'The Casio,' I go on. 'The broken one in your pocket.' Peter freezes for a second, then fumbles in his pocket. He gives me the watch; I hand him the photocopy. Seems like a fair deal: one tawdry, clapped-out token in exchange for another. A fake tenner for a busted Casio. But I say to myself: you're trying to buy time. To buy time off, to stop it running away. I know this gesture is as futile as my fantastic imaginings about Peter and me together. I know the battery on the Casio will run out in a few months, a year at most. Will I have the courage, when the digits on the display start to fade and flicker, to sling it straight in the bin?

A moment later Peter's on his way out through the front door. Just in time I call him back. 'This is for free,' I say, taking a deep breath. I lean over and kiss him full on the lips.

But this time he's gone. For good. Though it's late and it'll take me hours, I decide to set off back up north straight away. I scarcely give the house a backward glance. By the time I hit the M4 the tears are in full flow, I'm driving in the fast lane doing eighty, howling like a dog, weeping in great wrenching spasms. Like puking up uncontrollably. Don't give a shit if I kill myself in the process. Pathetic. Basket case. Sad old crone. I blank out completely along the A449, lose all track of time and place. Might as well be sleepwalking. Sleepdriving.

Just before I join the M50 my mobile starts ringing, jolts me back into life. I pull into a lay-by, compose myself the best I can, stammer into the mouthpiece. It's Peter. Says he can't bear to see me leave so suddenly. He was going to ask me to pop round, maybe go out for a drink, but as I'm obviously on the way home perhaps we'd better forget it. I tell him to give me an hour. Turn the car round, make it back to Ton in three quarters.

We spend a couple of hours in the pub. Talking. We cover politics, poetry, the cultural significance of Cerys Matthews and many other things. He lets slip that Chloe is sleeping over at her friend's house tonight. He'd forgotten to mention it earlier. Would I fancy a coffee?

As soon as we're through his front door I make my move. He responds in kind, his hands know exactly where I want them to go, gentle and transgressive in equal measure. There are two beautiful blonde acoustic guitars on the sofa, one almost finished, the other minus strings. Peter removes them carefully, gives each a light caress before laying them on the fraying Berber carpet. I sink into the sofa. As he leans across to kiss me, I notice the gratifying absence of extruding nose hairs.

'OK, Comrade,' I say, reaching for the top button of his jeans, 'let's see what you're made of.' And I think, I knew this guy once who reckoned he'd been wearing the same Casio digital for ten years, and it was still going strong.

A real bullshitter, he was, full of tall stories.

Just like me.

That's all. Thank you for listening.
My name's Judith Edwards.

# HELLO

## Ken Barlow

**Ken Barlow** was born in 1977 in Japan, then from the age of ten months brought up in St. Asaph, North Wales. He studied a BA in English & American Literature at Manchester University before staying on to do an MA in Novel Writing. He currently works in a bookshop and is writing a novel.

## April 1st, 8.15pm

There's an argument going on downstairs. I can hear it through the floor of my flat. They've been arguing a lot recently. Sometimes I try and drown it out by turning up the TV, or the stereo. Sometimes I listen. Tonight I'm listening. They're really going at it. Shouting. Screaming. Banging.

### April 1st, 9.36pm

She's left. A crescendo of screaming, a slammed door, and she's gone. I can hear the man downstairs muttering to himself. Swearwords, I think. He's stomping around so hard I can feel the floor vibrate. It makes me nervous. I turn on the TV.

### April 1st, 10.15pm

There's music exploding through the floor. Guitar, bass, drums thicken the air. It began about a minute ago, making me jump. The man downstairs must have a good stereo. A *great* stereo. Turned up full. I've heard him play his music before, but never *this* loud. I wonder what he's doing?

**April 1st, 10.16pm**

I think I recognise the song. I'm sure I do. What can it be?

**April 1st, 10.17pm**

Stinks Like Teen Sweat! By Banana! (I think).

**April 1st, 10.18pm**

It is, definitely. Not the sort of thing I'd usually listen to. I like Frank Sinatra. A bit of Andy Williams. But I remember this song from the radio. I hum along, slapping my palms against my thighs in time to the music. Didn't the singer shoot himself? Kit Something? I can't remember.

**April 1st, 10.20pm**

The room descends into silence. I feel disappointed. I'd like to hear the song again.

**April 1st, 10.20pm (+ 3 seconds)**

The song begins again. I turn the TV off, straining to listen. It's a good song. Full of life and energy. I stand up and jig around the room, waving my hands in the air.

**April 1st, 10.26pm**

The song finishes. I sit down.

**April 1st, 10.26pm (+ 3 seconds)**

The song begins again. I frown, puzzled. Why is he playing the song three times in a row? He must really like it. I lie back on the sofa, listening. I don't feel like getting up this time. The music is loud. Very loud. The sofa vibrates.

### April 1st, 10.32pm

The song finishes. The sofa is still.

### April 1st, 10.32pm (+ 3 seconds)

The song begins again. It's starting to irritate me now. The trembling sofa as well. I turn the TV back on. It's a soap opera. The people are shouting, but not loud enough. The music drowns them out. I turn the volume up, stabbing the remote button until my thumb hurts. Still not loud enough. I can't follow what's going on. He must have a really good stereo.

### April 1st, 10.38pm

The song stops. Is this the end?

### April 1st, 10.38pm (+ 3 seconds)

No. Again. Fifth time. Is it louder? It seems louder. I give up on the TV, throwing the remote control to the floor. It splits open, spilling the batteries. I get up, pick up the batteries, put them back in the remote, put it on the arm of the sofa. The song is in its chorus now. I can hear the words. Or one word repeated. *Hellohellohellohellohellohellohellohellohellohellohello...* I want it to stop.

### April 1st, 10.44pm

The song stops. One second, two seconds, three seconds-

### April 1st, 10.44pm (+ 3 seconds)

The song begins again. Every square inch of the room is filled, every atom vibrating to its beat. I pace around the room, searching for a nook or cranny to escape the sound. I stand in all four corners, one at a time, facing the wall, shutting my eyes. It makes no difference. *Hellohellohellohellohellohellohellohellohello...*

### April 1st, 10.50pm

The silence aches. I sit bolt upright, waiting, hoping...

### April 1st, 10.50pm (+ 3 seconds)

The song begins again. Seventh time? Eighth time? I'm losing count. I get up and stomp round the room, slamming my feet hard on the floor, hoping he'll hear. He doesn't, or does and chooses to ignore it. I stop in the centre of the room, leap high in the air and bring both feet down together. *Thump!* *Hellohellohellohellohellohellohellohellohello...* I pick up my worn, chipped cricket bat, propped against the bed in case of intruders, and swing it over my head like a mallet. Bang. Bang. *Bang!*

### April 1st, 10.56pm

Silence. Did he hear the banging? Has he stopped? Or...

### April 1st, 10.56pm (+ 3 seconds)

The song begins again. Why is he doing this? *Why?* Is it to get at me? But I've never argued with him. Never offended him (as far as I know). Barely ever spoken to him. I consider going downstairs, knocking on his door, having it out. But he's just had an argument with his girlfriend. He'll be upset. Angry. He might not listen to reason. He's a big man. With a shaved head. Perhaps even a scar. Best to leave him alone for now. He'll stop soon. He'll have to.

### April 1st, 11.26pm

It's inside my skull, buzzing round like a trapped fly. *Hellohellohellohellohellohellohellohellohello...* I've tried remaining calm. I've tried ignoring it. But now it's inside my skull. I even hate the silences, my three seconds (I've counted them) of escape. I cling to those three seconds, desperate for them to stretch into infinity. They never do. In a fit of anger, I pick up my stereo, a cheap little portable, and place it on the floor, speakers face down. Pressing play, I twist the volume dial up as far as it will go. The muffled sound of New York New York blares out. Immediately it is swallowed by the music downstairs. I kick the stereo in frustration and stub my toe. The pain is sharp, stabbing. I think I've broken it. I pick up the stereo and fling it against the wall. It splits open, vomiting out the CD.

### April 2nd, 12.00am

It's midnight now. I want to go to sleep. I step into my little bathroom/toilet with its mouldy, peeling walls, and brush my teeth, trying to ignore the music. I wash my face with soap and water, trying to ignore the music. I take a piss, trying to ignore the music. I flush the toilet, trying to lose myself in the whirlwind whoosh! of water. But still the music's there, trapped inside my skull. *Hellohellohellohellohellohellohellohello...*

### April 2nd, 12.21am

Wrapped up tight beneath the covers of my bed I close my eyes and try to ignore the vibrations. *(I can see the music!)* Panting, scared, my eyes flick open. A strange chill grips me. It's a full minute before I dare to close them again. *I can see the music!* A squirming blob of discordant sound, pulsating insanely like a maddened heart. I bury my head in the pillow. It feels like it is going to explode. The music is everywhere. In the room, in the bed, in my skull. I want to *sleep*.

### April 2nd, 2.17am

Push! Straining, grunting, I try to shit the music out of me. *Push!* I can feel a vein throbbing in my forehead. *Push!* The plastic toilet seat feels cold against my arse. *Push!* It's no use. I slump, burying my head in my hands. The music is caught in my bowels, a constipated lump of melody. I'm tired. I start to sob, tears dampening my palms. I'm *tired*.

### April 2nd, 4.04am

Why is he doing this? Spite? Anger? Vengeance? Why? I'm trembling, my skin covered in a slimy film of sweat. I writhe about the bed, limbs pushed into crooked, unnatural angles. The music is in control, twining its chords round my fingers and toes, tossing me about like a mannequin. I try to stop, to lie still, to sleep. But I can't. Why is he doing this? *Why?*

### April 2nd, 5.16am

I'm walking round in circles, legs like jelly. It's as if all my bones have disappeared, leaving only soft, sloppy flesh. I can barely keep moving. The circles are concentric, becoming ever smaller, until I'm stood in the centre of the room, naked. Rooted to the spot, the music crawls up my legs, shoots up my throat, explodes inside my skull. *Hellohellohellohellohellohellohellohellohello...* I drop to the floor, kneeling on hands and knees, shouting, 'Shut up!' *Hello-* 'Not hello! *Not* hello!' *Hellohello-* 'Goodbye goodbye goodbye!' *Hellohellohello-* I pound my fists against the floor, saliva dripping from my lips.

### April 2nd, 6.39am

I'm so tired I dream I'm asleep. For a few sweet seconds I think I'm gone. Escaped into a blissful world of sleep. Then I realise it's a sham. I'm awake, in Hell, eyeball deep in music. It's strange. I feel torn between two worlds. Or lost in the void between. My mind is disintegrating, crumbling like weathered rock.

### April 2nd, 7.01am

Stranger still. I feel weightless, as if made of air. Any second now I'm going to float up, up, and away. I look at my hand and it seems blurred, transparent. I can see the wall through it, see the cracks in the plaster. I'm fading away. The music is distant now, spilling out of the hollow left behind. I'm going, going...

### April 2nd, 7.17am

Gone. The first fragile light of dawn spills across the room. But it's empty, still as the Marie Celeste. I'm drifting round the room, lighter than air. Somewhere below, I hear music. Loud music. It draws me toward it, like a moth to a flame. I float downward, breezing effortlessly through the floor. I'm in a room with a stereo. A big, black stereo. It plays a song, stuck on repeat, the volume so loud it shakes the walls. In the centre of the room is a wooden chair, knocked on its side. Suspended above it, a leather belt wrapped round his neck, hangs a man. A big man, with a shaved head. And a scar. I drift above him, below him, through him. Touching his pale face with ghostly hands, I gaze into his milky eyes and mouth a single, silent word...

'Hello.'

# A SORT OF HOMECOMING

Tristan Hughes

**Tristan Hughes** was born in Atikokan, Canada, where he lived for two years before moving to Wales. Educated at David Hughes School, Menai Bridge, the universities of York and Edinburgh, and King's College, Cambridge, he has recently completed a thesis on Pacific and American travel literature. He currently lives in Anglesey.

It flashes into view, hard and clear like waking, after the winding, cocooning green of the bends. The point is called Gallows. Masts are packed in the air over beached boats, a confusion of crosses, clicking, tinkling, whirring in the breeze; mad clockwork sounds that measure a chaos of time that runs not just forwards but backwards and sideways too. Cross-winds. Ropes hang everywhere, rocking like nooses. From the point (of no return, he can't go back now, can't run from this or here) the sea wall curves gently inwards while opposite, across the straits, the mountains bulge outwards into the horizon and are reflected down into the sea as though the whole scene is made out of mirrors. Seagulls swoop in distorted space towards the summits of the mountains in the sea. On the other side of the little bay the shore is a bright phalanx of colour where a Georgian terrace laps the water, painted pink and yellow and green; candy houses with marzipan walls and icing roofs, like those gaudy, confectionery cottages in fairy tale woods that lost and orphan children look hungrily towards.

*

"There's a message for you Robert, I think its kind of urgent." His boss retreats instantly, the onerous task performed, meandering past computers and their cables that sprawl, disemboweled, across the floor. Robert Llewelyn looks down towards his screen: "In *De-Scribing The Savage* Professor Larkin, one of America's finest critics, offers both a brilliant analysis of the colonial discourse on savagery and a major contribution to post-colonial theory. Concentrating on the textual representation of encounter Larkin unravels the ..." He feels himself unraveling, as he has felt for years now, stretched and dislocated as though all the hyphens he has had to re-scribe in these fucking blurbs has hyphenated him. Yes, I'm Ro-bert, very good to meet you. They always give him this stuff to do. Ato, who works in the same office, is half Nigerian but they think it might be too obvious if they handed it to him, stereotyping: give the black guy the colonial material, he's sure to be interested. They're still a bit guilty for it all he sees - sorry about our empire fucking up your country, we feel terrible about it, we know better now. But as for a Llewelyn, well that happened seven hundred years ago, who even remembers, lots of time to get over it. Only a name, not even a skin, to remind them of ancient borders overthrown. To remind himself. They like it at dinner parties, it's a good conversation starter: "Llewelyn, that's Welsh isn't it ... You are ...Where from ...Can you pronounce that place with the really long name?" A hint of ethnicity, very fashionable in London now. Savage, from the French souvage, a dweller in woods and forests; wild, uncultivated. When he first arrived he didn't know how to use the underground or what wine to buy or where exactly Soho was. Everyone was surprised he wasn't even more of a hick. Barbarian, from the Greek barbaros, to babble, meaning those who do not speek Greek. "Llanfair-pwll-gwyngych ....", low murmurings of amusement ripple into the room as the impacted double l's and rasped ch's dance through the air like performers in a circus.

There is a small memo pad in the corner of the room with one line scrawled upon it. Nobody is around, they have left him alone with this. He reads it slowly, trying to make it last: "Robert, can you phone home immediately - your father has passed away." It is the full stop he notices most, thinking how he has never really felt a full stop before. They have helped him catch his breath but they have never taken his breath away. A life drifts around him in the room, his own, his fathers', pieced together with a less harsh punctuation, a dash here and there, the odd semicolon, a mix of exclamation and question marks; clauses that seem to run on forever and forever ... And then this little dot stares up at him, prohibiting extension, whispering that syntax isn't going to help him here, that grammar is full of what is lost and irredeemable. It is a cruel sentence to be handed. It is.

Outside on the street the letters on the signs seem to have lost their coherence, their fixity, and returned to some primordial condition where they are just strange shapes stuck together. The alphabet has exploded and lies strewn in charred fragments all around. Everything is unraveling now and beneath it all is death. What did they expect? What did he expect?

*

Past the candy houses and around the corner and he has arrived. Castle Street is bustling beneath drooping banners that proclaim some town festival, looking exhausted with the burden of civic happiness they bear. A torn poster on the window of Edith's Newsagents announces that there will be a Lithuanian jazz quartet playing at the Bulkley Hotel on Thursday, followed by Misty Twilight, 'a world renowned' four piece Celtic rock band. Looking down the sidewalk Robert wonders if this might all be too much for the slow-bobbing blue rinses that hover everywhere on the verge of the road, perched, as if on the very edge of eternity, while they wait for the traffic to recede so they may cross over to the Castle bakery and buy 'authentic Welsh raison bread'. They come all year, shipped along in gleaming metallic tubes - Fringe Express, World's End Motors, Dragon Coaches - sealed off from the attritional, scouring rains and winds that arrive interminably from the Irish Sea; they have little left, more to preserve. Pensioners from everywhere, mostly women - the men die earlier - come to look at the castle as though it offered some vision of corresponding decay, of crumbling, rock-strewn endurance. He had grown up pushing impatiently between them and, returning, notices a faint aroma in the place that he has forgotten, an invisible patina that floats like scum upon the air, the scent of composty earth and slithery autumn leaves; a detritus of perished cells - the smell they have left over. Twilight: everywhere it is misting through their eyes, the light failing, falling, beneath it is ... He is home.

Robert has not been back for years. Not since he began to feel his life spinning out of the orbit he had imagined it following, become sidetracked in an unmapped constellation that he knows now is failure, where the starlight shines at different angles as though viewed from some other hemisphere. This readjustment in space has made him shifty, furtive, a guilty interloper in the place where his dreams had formed. Coming back he feels a traitor, a betrayer of some earlier self that had formed out of this small island world a promise of undefinable vastness - of tundras, steppes, prairies - that would pulse and tremble behind the hedgerows and fields and houses and sky. That prior self and the quivering landscape that surrounds it will not leave him now, even in London, they are like an albatross hanging upon him, a hanging judge. What he has been and what he is are two places, two countries; borders that will not be broken. Outside Evans' Funeral Parlour he sees John and Bev Roberts and ducks away down Church Street to avoid meeting them. It's a reflex action, the traitor's instinct: avoid eye-contact, speaking, explanation, they might see it in your eyes, hear it in your voice. He knew their daughter Tracy in school, they were friends, lovers too he remembers now. Why are they here? Her grandmother, he thinks, looking back a decade to a liver-coloured old woman who lurked in a house, upstairs, an inconvenience to them both. He waits for them to walk past and prepares to see his father.

Mr. Evans, tender of the town's dead, meets him at the front of the parlour. Inside it is slatey-cool, refrigerated by a cold stone through which the spring sun cannot obtrude. "This must be a terrible time for you Robert, coming out of the blue like that. Nobody could have expected it." Evans speaks with professional graveness, the voice gently assuaging an unspoken indictment: he died alone, he died without you here, why didn't you visit all these years? His father had nobody else, no other family in a family country. Robert's mother had died in childbirth and become an invisible woman who lived in the melancholy glinting of his father's eye. There were no aunties and uncles and cousins. They came from meager stock his people, barrens; producing even him had been too much, a fatal taxing of their paltry fertility. He thinks of this often during sex, imagines the deficient rush of his briny sperm as though it were some dead sea tributary trickling by in sterile, salty streams, not coming but departing. "You must have made good time to get back so quickly," says Evans, making small talk as they walk towards the room where the body is stored, the pronunciation careful, camouflaging the other language that lies behind it, the other accusations: why did you leave us, why did you forget what was yours? Evans knows that Robert has lost much of his father's first tongue. Does it matter now? he thinks. Surely the dead cannot speak any language. There can be no bilingualism to link those in the grave with the living. Alone with his father, in a cold room full of slightly chemical smells that remind him of dissecting frogs in school, Robert is shocked by the silence. In his memory there is noise everywhere: the crackling, spluttering sounds of fat boiling in his dad's chippy (what will he do with it now); the drunken, exaggerated loudness of the lads jostling around the counter on Saturdays; the gruff hwyl of farmers come by for a mid-week treat of oozing, oily sglodions; the droning of an old radio set amongst plastic bottles of sauce and vinegar. His father is at the centre of all this noise, sharp-eyed and watchful, thick eyebrows arching over gleaming metallic edges that frame glass cases in which lie crusted slabs of fish, shriveled lengths of sausage, flaking pies. He is waiting in that noise, always waiting, for what Robert could never guess. Maybe for his wife to return, to materialise out of the frying, fat-sparkling air, her bones once more coated in a batter of pink, living flesh. Or maybe he had simply been waiting for the noise to stop. He had been a farmer's boy and never forgot the corner of land his father had sold to buy the shop, the quiet fields he had worked as a child with only the rushing wind around him. He had been most cheerful on those Saturday afternoons when the farmers came to sell him potatoes, arriving in rickety vans and unloading coarse, bulging brown bags that smelt of fresh earth, moist and fecund. They would stand together at the back door, speaking raucously in Welsh, elated by the small harvest that sat on the pavement. Afterwards his father would linger by the open sacks, inhaling the scent of clinging dirt like it was a perfumed emissary from paradise. They were his link with the patch of ground where he had been happiest, where his wife had not died, where his son would not leave.

The skin on his father's face looks waxed and pallid as though covered by a layer of cold, congealed grease, and Robert half expects to catch the familiar aroma of stale chip fat drifting towards him. But there is nothing, there is not even the grief he felt welling within him when he first read the note. His father died then, this body is no confirmation, no accentuation of that moment; death cannot be extended, even by a body, its leftovers. The features are almost the same as when he left: the high cheekbones, the drooping nose, the little heart of a mouth. He has aged well. Only the slackness of the skin along the jaw and the extra layer of collapsed flesh beneath the chin acknowledge the intervening years, but perhaps that is what happens to corpses. How should he know, this is the first he has seen. In the stone-chill of the room he feels the desire to hide slip away, his betrayal is safe with his father, entombed. The past is comfortable here, with the dead. Suddenly he is a boy again, wandering along the shore of the small bay, picking his way through twisted clumps of seaweed, looking out onto the winking scintillation of the straits and the mountains beyond which loom darkly and flare into green luminescence as the clouds scud over the sun, a panorama of swift shadow and light. The world is hovering, fluttering like a hummingbird's wing, its airy transparency irradiated by some great immanent space in which his heart expands until it is huge, until it could almost break. A promise, a secret, a revelation, given to him by this little postage-stamp in the sea, that he carried with him always, that he went away that he might learn to translate it, to return it as a gift of thanks, but instead let wither and fade, finding in its vacated place an emptiness of unspeakable, mute vastness, a world in which he will always be lost. The cold eyelids of his father stare up at him. "I'm sorry," he whispers, tears wetting his lips, "I am sorry fy nhad."

\*

Inside The George the afternoon has been hidden behind musky floral curtains. Jack Tacsi and Doreen are sitting in the corner beside an empty fireplace fringed by brass ornaments that look dull and pallid, yearning for the absent flames to light them. They look up and see Robert at the bar, sloshing a pint of Stella with hands that are trembling; it has been a difficult day and he cannot shed the coldness of Evans's parlour from his skin. "Rob lad," calls Jack, "wot the fokk are you doing back?" Rumbled at last Robert walks nervously over to join them, steeling himself to hide his failure once more. But after a few pints it has retreated, receded into some distant corner that is another country, far away from here. Jack and Doreen are reminiscing about Rob's old man and slowly, as the appropriate, comforting earnestness with which death introduces itself begins to fade into familiarity, they begin to laugh together. Jack is telling a story about how he and Rob's father had collected a load of fish in his old van and stopped off at the Sailors Arms for a quick one, which became a quick eight or nine, after which they forgot about the van and staggered off leaving the fish to the mercy of the hottest August day anyone could remember." ...it wos fokkin stinkin like a bastard when we went back, I'm tellin ya, you could smell it in fokkin Llanfairfechan ...". Jack's face is alive with laughing, though the years of drinking have puckered it inwards, like the vortex of water that is sucked finally down the plughole. He had once skippered a charter fishing boat that trolled tourists out past Puffin Island and into the ocean. Robert remembers its name, Starider, and imagines Jack at its helm plunging through a sea of stars. They are in his beer now, percolating silver orbs floating in a golden milky way, stellar, a beautiful space where time is stilled and softened, it binds them here - him, Jack, Doreen - they are watching the stars from the same place. "Did you hear about Tracy Roberts," Doreen asks, taking silence as an answer, "poor thing was killed in a car crash about three days ago." The heavens are shifting again, nothing will stop them.

Outside he knows where he is going. Down the street and around past the castle walls that stand in crumbling watchfulness, looking out into the surrounding woods that have receded over the centuries into long fields dotted with vestigial oaks; this ancient anglo-island put up to keep its eye upon the unruly natives that lurked beyond its perimeters, behind the trees, babbling in an alien tongue. He walks up the sloping fields towards the undiminished clusters of forest that still remain, passing beneath the shadows of the single, lonely, leftover oaks. They had hidden in these little cocoons of green once, Tracy and him, finding refuge here from the liver-coloured presence of the grandmother. They had lain on the gentle, leafy grass, her black hair falling about above his head, the slight chill of evening upon them, damp and dewy, and then the sudden hot wetness of her, almost stinging him, enclosing him in a moment of frantic, slippery warmth. Afterwards the slight sadness, the intimation of a small emptiness returning, the light fading under the cushioning branches. "Did you come in me?" she had whispered here. "Yes," he had said, "I came." She has gone now. Somewhere, he thinks, her body lies crumpled and broken. Perhaps beside his father's. He digs his fingers into the earth, gathering it in his hand and pressing it into his face, tasting its fecund decay, smelling its bountiful rotting. Twilight is descending now, covering him, and below the town is dissolving in an evening mist; the castle walls, the dreaming, delicious houses, the tranced water, the still and silent masts, the mountains insubstantial as clouds, all are dispersing into a vapoury darkness, hanging on the borders of night.

# THE POINT

## Deborah Davies

**Deborah Davies** has recently completed a PhD, and was, until May 2002, a creative writing tutor at Cardiff University. She is currently preparing to publish her first collection of short stories, which include many that have appeared individually. Her fiction has been broadcast on Radio 4 and published in MsLexia magazine. She has been a prize-winner in the last two Rhys Davies short story competitions. She writes poetry using the name Deborah Chivers.

I want to tell about the feel of my new clothes on a Sunday
school anniversary morning. One year I had a chocolate brown
dress, and I loved the colour. I loved everything about that dress
with its six layers of stiff, dark petticoat underneath. Cool layers
crackling like wrapping paper that made me feel like a present, and
how the layers insinuated themselves sweetly between my thighs,
and the way those petticoats lay in rough panels of chocolate lace
all around me; a satisfaction of dark, lumpy lace over bouncing
underthings and the wide sash holding it all in, safe, around my
seven-year-old waist.

There was an American redcurrant bush in our front
garden, its smell dried out the insides of your nose; those bitter
leaves, hairy and ridged. And my father with the camera, taking
photos of me in the hot garden. Stand with the flowers behind
you, sweet, he'd said, stand still as you can. And I stood like a
small, lacy statue for my father. I would have stood all day, in my
holy dress, my hair uncurling, drooping, in spite of my mother
who'd worked with curlers and sprays. My mother who stood like
a navy and white column and waited, a smile wavering across her
pretty face, for us to be ready. I would have been happy to stand
with the tender ends of the redcurrant bush resting on my
shoulders and the purple flowers falling like miniature bunches of
grapes bump-bumping my hair. My smooth hair I could feel
relaxing its curls in the sunshine and silence. All for my father to

71

say to me good, good, and one more, this one will be beautiful.

I want to tell about my sister, four years old, who, unnoticed, sat in the garden dust and smudged her peach anniversary dress. How I was replete with a secret gladness to see her dress was dirty and she could not have her picture taken. My sister's hair had a cow's lick fringe that never would stay flat, no matter how my mother tried with brushes and clips and water. And how someone yanked her up out of the dust so that she fell and cut her knee, the cut looking so bright and raw against the warm frills and fall of her dress. So out of place; the worm of blood that worked its way down her leg and soaked her new white sock, collecting in a dark stain. And my legs, no scabs, but one bruise on my shin. I remember how I got that bruise; the smell of the hot, thunderous pavement I tripped on after a sudden shower of raindrops, heavy and shocking as an undeserved smack.

Often I would lie awake at night, long before I shared the bedroom, and run my hand over the wall from where I lay in bed. My arm described an arc, my thin arm with longish blond hair and a click in the elbow. The wallpaper was warm and felty, patterned with sprigs of roses and buds. Each bud had a spiteful face that stared out from behind a leaf. I enjoyed wetting the bed in that twilit room full of bird-song and spiteful faces. I waited in the warm, spreading patch I'd made in the bedclothes for my mother to climb the stairs and loom through the door. Hanging on the back of the door there was a deep-red dressing gown with a tassel tie. In the dark when the streetlights were out the dressing gown turned black and writhed. Then I listened for the sounds of my parents downstairs, each clink of china and chime of cutlery like a soothing pat on my cheek, lying there in the dark.

My father would run, each step so light, up the stairs after I'd thought about him long and hard enough. And when he was with me in my room he made it different; better. Shut your eyes, he'd say, and open your hands, and then he'd place a biscuit or a piece of heavy gingerbread or sometimes a cube of salty cheese in my palms. And the times he pulled my toes until the joints clicked, although my mother told him mildly no, you'll spoil her feet, you monster. Does it hurt? She always asked. I would offer my toes to my father, and my fingers for him to bite. She likes me doing it, he'd say, not looking her way. He'd smile at me, whispering, you do, don't you darling? My father had a black and white checked jacket with leather patches on the elbows and leather trim around the cuffs. It had an amber smell of wood, tobacco and mints. If I breathed that smell everything was going to be all right, always.

I want to tell about my mother who was twenty-six for so long. How she talked to herself, nodding and smiling as she washed up and looked out of the window through the trees towards the mountain. She licked her pencil tip before she wrote a shopping list. In the evening when she took her apron off and combed out her fluffy, pale hair; don't touch my hair she'd say, it's a thing I can't stand. You didn't have to touch her hair to know how soft it was. It smelt of sandalwood and fresh ironing. In the evening she sat like someone who'd had the air extracted from inside. She said, I wish a little sprite would come and do the washing up for me. She'd say this in a dreamy voice. Look at my lovely feet she'd say, and lift them up slightly, the arches extreme, her toes so perfect. You haven't inherited my feet, poor thing, she'd say, take off your socks. And yes, my feet were thin, different, not nearly as nice as my mother's small, plump feet.

I had a doll as a present for no particular reason from my beautiful, beehive-haired, buck-toothed auntie, who had glasses with wings at the sides, who wore diamonds and had long red nails. She had pointy ankle-turning shoes that scraped their metal heel tips on the path and sprayed sparks as she walked. My doll I named Valerie had coarse, platinum hair and lips so small they looked as if she disapproved. But I knew this wasn't so. One day my sister poked out Valerie's unblinking blue eyes with the point of a compass; blinded Valerie for life. My mother said here, good as new, and turned Valerie's eyes full circle so the pink backs were at the front, and drew new eyes for her with a brown felt-pen. Then her eyes were brown and crooked and the way she looked at me with those brown eyes, I knew she was a different person, and I stuffed her in the back of the cupboard, beside the yellow tartan kilt, behind the piles of crusts and other things I didn't want to eat.

Then my mother said to my sister, come here, bad girl, and say sorry. And she did, squeezing her arms hard around my waist, butting me with her head until I fell over backwards. There, friends again, said my mother; you forgive her don't you? Then she turned back to the washing up. My mother's blond hair glowed like a halo, her lips moved, eyebrows lifting, as she talked soundlessly to the mountain through the window. I can't explain how much I loved my doll Valerie, how she was the only doll I ever wanted. Each time I thought about her squashed up in the cupboard I wanted to do something, but I couldn't decide what.

One summer morning I woke up and knew that something special was going to happen. Something that would change everything forever. I could hardly wait for the day to begin. Later on in the morning I thought perhaps I had been wrong. Then, in the afternoon, when the heat was so heavy it had choked the birds into silence, my mother called us out to where she was resting under the apple-tree at the bottom of the garden. She lay in a deck chair with her feet resting on a stool, flicking through magazines. She was wearing a strappy pink top tied with a knot at the front. The air was cool and green under the tree, gold patches moved about on mother's pale skin. In the grass by her side she had a clear drink, full of blobs of ice. I want to tell how her voice sounded as she told us to go out to play; drowsy and mild. Now girlies, don't come back for at least an hour, she said. Stay together. And remember, she said, holding me gently by the wrist, you're the oldest, so take good care. We stood by the side of the lounger, not wanting to go. Wanting to watch our mother resting and quiet, it was so odd. Shoo, she said, buzz, and waved us away, her wrist in a beautiful droop.

I ran across the field outside our house and tried to lose my sister but she clung on. Down by the stream it was shady. There were clumps of shining watercress and some plants with big hairy leaves that smelt of mint. I made my sister eat them. I told her she must eat twelve leaves. They could be poisonous, I said. You've got to trust me. I watched her chewing on the sappy leaves. Her lips puckered and green spittle collected in the corners of her mouth. It was dim, like a cave down there amongst the tall ferns.

I started to climb a big beech tree I knew well. I told my sister it was too hard for her to climb, but she still followed. I could hear her puffing and scrabbling as she tried to keep up with me. For someone so small she was a good climber; she never got scared. Soon we were nearly at the top and stopped to rest. I sat back against the trunk of the tree and looked at my sister as she nestled on a branch. She breathed quietly but deeply. She was pleased to be so high up, I knew. I could see down through the fine mesh of trembling, veiny leaves to the little brown stream and the undergrowth. I could feel the ridgy skin of the tree through my blouse. My sister looked perfectly at home. Her chin was clotted with green saliva, the flesh underneath her eyes shining with sweat.

I lunged forward and pushed her hard off the tree. I sat and gripped the trunk, listening to her body crash and thump down through the branches. She didn't scream. Then there was silence. I want to tell what it was like sitting in the tree trying to hear the sound of my sister settling in the bushes far below me. A dog barked and I started to climb down. My limbs were aching and wouldn't work properly. I fell the last few feet and hurt my side. I heard my skirt rip.

She wasn't near the bottom of the tree. I searched the undergrowth and saw a scrap of gingham. I forced myself through the blackberry bushes and ivy. My arms and legs were stinging from the bramble thorns. She was still. Lying face down. One of her shoes was missing, her sock was hanging halfway off, her bare heel had a pearly sheen. Her hair was a little crown standing out. Lying there she looked like a different person. I had to turn her. I did it with my foot. She made a sound as she rolled over onto her back; half a sigh, half my name. She had a sharp beech twig, maybe six inches long, impaled in her blue, blue eye. I don't know how far it went inside. I don't think very far. Blood was pooling. There were some torn, lime-green leaves on the twig. Her unhurt eye was moving. I think she was looking for me.

# LOVE'S LIGATURE

## Dennis Lewis

**Dennis Lewis** is a feminist, a chauvinist and a contradiction in terms. He is a recovering alcoholic, an enraged cuckold and a closet wig-wearer. Barely literate, his muddy prose wallows in self-pity, face-lifted clichés, tautologies and weary metaphor. His favourite colour is avocado.

They say that talking to yourself is a bad sign. I was not only talking to myself, I was having arguments with myself, full blown rows. I sometimes got so angry with myself that I ended up not talking to myself for days on end. So instead of talking to myself, I'm going to try to write it down, because if I write it down it may make sense: it may mean something.

I thought he'd be back by now. After a month, two months; I thought he'd be back. Like when you wave away a wasp from a can of pop, I thought – he'll come back; they always do, don't they. They always come back...don't they? Still no letter. Only the junk. It arrives effortlessly, fuel-lessly; without a trace of sweat or the post-man's uncomplaining hand: it's just banged through the door.

Junk mail. It stirs the early morning realm of the hallway with particles of dust; the light-scorched motes of morning. It flutters to the floor with the surprised whiteness of sea-gull wings; the specialist flutter of envelopes that stretches the fragility of twanging nerves. I can't bear the noise of the snapping, spring-loaded mouth of the door, spreading all that useless paper around the hall like a child has just finished amusing itself. My eyes are always searching for the human scrawl, the friendly curve of ink, his familiar hand. Searching for warmth, for reconciliation, searching even for an empty page - the silence of forgiveness. Anything. But there is nothing; only the junk. And the bills.

Since my husband left, the post has been full of torture, it's been full of tragic stories. I really don't need it, it's all gone so wrong. The trouble is I don't have enough money; we always had enough when he was working, it was never a jackpot but it was enough. Now I can't bear to open the bills. The plea of poverty is no defence against the demands, the begging for payment: the threats. I grow pale at the sight of all those bleeding figures and columns; the incarnadine numbers of warning: the sanguinary ciphers of disconnection.

I've noticed that the first thing I do when I open a bill is burst into hysterical laughter. You just can't take it seriously. It's a psychopathic thing: you just have to go nuts every time you open a bill. I hate not having enough money; it's so stressful. How can people stand it - it's so...so annihilating. I'd love to have a job, but what could I do? What could I *do*? I've learned that without a job you're poor. And I just can't afford to be poor - being poor is just too damned expensive.


Poverty arrived like an accident; suddenly and painfully. Poverty arrived when Gerald left. No that's not exactly true, it happened before. It happened a year ago. He'd lost his job, became depressed, then he left...no...he didn't leave, he ran away. Scared. He was scared that I'd stopped loving him. After twenty-five years of marriage he ran away...dear God it was twenty-five years! He was Logistics Manager when the company went bankrupt. He'd worked for them since leaving school. Oh, there was no money when they closed the place down. You know, he cried like a baby when they told him. Every molecule of him was shell-shocked. When he came home he couldn't talk, he just cried. He cried a lot after that, but at least he'd do it quietly. He'd go and stand in the garden and when he came in his eyes would be red and swollen.

He used to be so strong. When he was working he always seemed in control - all white shirt and pie-charts. How could he just stand around crying like that? Why couldn't he get out and *do* something? Anyway, after a year of unemployment, he ran away.

He told me that I didn't love him because he couldn't get a job, because he was useless. There were no hysterics, no valedictory argument. That's all he said; then he walked out. The next day, I found his note; his dagger shaped missive. The white enveloped cliché was an exultant bayonet. She was a 'darling woman' and 'it had to be'; then at last came the stomach shredding boastfulness of, 'She loves me.'

He was right. My feelings for him had changed. It's true that nothing ever forbids love, though it's also true that poverty is a graveyard of buried love. It's easy to love the adored-one when they are hung with the trophies of gainful employment; a well paid job endears the heart of many a loved-one. But poverty outdoes love's patience. Poverty chokes love, becoming a ligature around love's vulnerable neck. I used to think that love was the all the weather-proofing we needed on the weft and warp of our lives. But love is porous: poverty passes through love. And then jealousy lowers morale even further. A person who is poor is constantly occupied with the possessions that other people have; the things that are forbidden to them. Like opening the post without going mental.

I have spent the last hour looking out of the kitchen window at the rain. An hour that dragged on longer than walking a silent mile. There are solid columns of rain shooting in inky jets out of the impatient hurry-up clouds. Constant rain has turned the streets into gloomy oceanic channels, like the deep crepuscular cut at Corinth. They have their own shipping lanes of ebbing and flowing traffic; their own spiteful currents of pushing-green and shoving-grey, their sediments of styrofoam, crushed cans and cigarette butts. They have their own Marie Celestes and Titanics, their 'shipwrecked' and 'lost souls'. The drowning pavements shimmer with dull light - I'm getting overwrought with Schadenfreude staring at the punished, pathetic, down-trodden streets. What happens in the last thrashing moments of those deluged pavements? Do their entire lives flash past: the fearful violence, the tearful partings, all the pain and shame of their entire trampled lives? Looking at the rain alone from a window is hard on the nerves; watching the dismal rain is so bloody...*dismal*. I hate the rain and I hate the ache I get from my life. I hate the kind of scared feeling I get when I think about how my world has disappeared; how it's all been nuked - that neutron kind of nuke that makes people disappear but leaves houses standing. He still doesn't phone. Still no letter. He keeps me standing naked in the cold.

I've been drinking quite a bit lately, though drink doesn't do anything for a dead life. It doesn't do anything for the pain of a dead life. The nights are thirstiest. I've tried vodka and gin and whisky. Whisky tastes so bad that I end up throwing the glass across the room. Then when I've drunk enough to be immune to the taste, I end up finishing the bottle. Drink doesn't help. It just explodes another gigabyte of memory and torches a few million liver cells. And then there's that morning after feeling - the repeated coshing of the hangover; the de-mythologizing bloody hangover. But perhaps just one more time. Just one more glass of anaesthesia, then maybe my mind can sew its absolving sutures of sleep.

There is a poet I know who lives nearby; in a flat above a takeaway. We met while walking in the park the other day. When I told him my husband had left me, he stopped in mid-stride and swore loudly and with some feeling. He told me that lots of people seemed to be doing that these days - leaving. It had happened to him: his wife had left him for another man. I swear I saw a sheen of tears in his eyes; they looked like skinned knuckles with their bright patina of pain. It's the eyes that give it away. They were life-faded, wept-out; they were on the run from a new existence, a heavier kind of gravity. Love-wounds never heal: the hot coal beneath the skin that never cools. Isn't there an important message here, a shattering emotional hieroglyph ? – Nothing is ours. Nothing is guaranteed.

After a while he took out a can of beer from a six-pack he carried and offered it to me. I said - no thanks, I was trying to keep a grip on it. When he sat on the grass to drink his beer, I said goodbye and walked away. He called after me...

'Don't worry. Everything will be ok in the end.' I raised a palm as I turned and walked on. It struck me that we were both travelling through the same vandalised time; the same burned out space: like two looping, shuddering worlds in the same catastrophically shifted orbit. We were like two slapped cheeks on the same stunned face.

I looked back at his hunched shape, curled like an ammonite over his beer can. He was sniffing at the smudged city air. He looked gouged and pinched - he looked poor too, in his exhausted denims and fluky black tee-shirt. I don't know what they pay poets these days, but it can't be much. No sir, no way - they can't be paying poets much at *all*. The poet had no money and no health; he was a money and health bankrupt: I could tell. The cliché-ridden wordster could really have done with a friendly arm around his shoulder. Who couldn't?

I stood gazing at this stereo-type, an idealised image of a poet: poor but unconquered, the lost song-bird singing into the storm with bird-sized bravery, the word magician struggling to wring rose-water from life's cesspool. I'm going to write to those constipated bastards down at the Arts Council - yes, and tell them to give more boodle to the poets. Yes - more loot to the poor unrewarded poets. I liked the verse-monger, but I wouldn't want to spent much time with him: our little talk had only succeeded in scrabbling our nerves and in stoking up the fever of our drink-thirsty rage.

This morning the hall was cheerfully empty, gleaming with cruel hilarity. Today there was nothing on the floor. No letter. No junk. I spent the day down at the coast staring at the ocean. The Atlantic's frisky shoulders tormented the defiant cliffs, whorling and slipping in foaming bravado across the sharp daggers of stone.

I spared a tender thought for the frenzied waves throwing themselves onto the rocks like the suicidal Japanese women of Saipan. The exhausted rock-torn water was merrily prancing and laughing, it's frothy amusement masking its injury. It seemed to be saying, 'It's not hurting. It's not hurting.' I watched the ocean for hours; it held me, reflected me. It said every-thing. It told the same lies.

Run up the flags! It's finally happened! I'm helpless with happiness - he's finally found his voice. At last my thought missile has struck home. He rang last night. I couldn't stop saying 'Yes...Yes...Yes.' Each thud of my heart was willing him to come home. His call has pushed the breath out of me. I'm in a light sweat. He's on his way. What will I say to him? Will he be ashamed? Should I be ashamed? Should I praise him for coming to his senses...what can I *sayeee*? I'm falling into a panic of self-consciousness, so I move from room to room trying to find something useful to do. I feel like lead, it's like my body weighs a ton. My God, I'm falling apart here. But I don't care - he's coming *hooome*! Coming to ruffle this mausoleum with his booming voice and flapping arms, to fill the bathroom with his croaky songs; to slide snugly into bed and hook a reassuring arm around me.

I tiptoe up to a mirror, and freeze. My skin is as blotchy as worn denim. My hair is unbrushed like a tousled dog, the creases in my neck are like velveteen ribbons. The face staring out of the mirror is as wrinkled and grey as the sodden streets. How ugly I've become, how heart-breakingly ugly I've become in the deep-lined whiteness of depression; that poisonous venom of poverty and defeat. The mirror seems to recoil into its dark backing: unbelieving, shocked, repudiating. I am a ruin - Ephesus, Delphi, the Sphinx - I am one. Was there ever beauty beneath the crumbling mortar? I watch the slits of my eyes begin to fill with tears; become fuming pools of stress and alcohol.

Much reconstruction is needed. You demolish, then you

reconstruct. A new face (you settle for less) then off you go again. The trouble it takes to preserve a nice face, tragic. Soon, the enlightened woman will begin a new epoch, preventing beauty abusing its powers. I look terrible. And I'm beginning to feel terrible...I feel like some writhing thing that lives at the bottom of a deep ocean; colourless and brittle. I need a drink. I need a lot of drink. I hear an extraordinary voice coming from behind my teeth; a megaphone voice shouting at me. I'm saying out loud - 'But he's on his way home. You don't need drink anymore. Be happy. Surely to God things will get better now?'

Ah yes, God...my pal God. Nietzsche, apparently, killed God. But I hope not. Maybe he didn't finish him off; maybe he just winged him: maybe it was just a flesh wound. Oh sure, God is down, and he's bleeding, but maybe he isn't finished off: not yet. And that's just like life too, isn't it? Just when you need God, just when you want him with his ear to the phone, someone takes a pot-shot at him - tries to assassinate him. I imagine God crouched in a corner of the mirror exhausted, too bloody tired to say a word. I've been keeping his particular hotline busy lately: God may not be kaput, but after all the running around he's been doing for me, he certainly must be at death's door.

I now know - it's not the money. Money isn't the problem. Having my life turn to doo-doo and flushed down the toilet is the problem. Having to wear shame and rejection like a lead coat is the problem. Expecting security is the problem too, when security took off a long time ago; it didn't have what it takes to stick around. Where do you see security anymore anyway? Nobody has any. Take it from me, don't look for security - learn how to handle change instead.

I've been scared witless since all this happened, but now I realise that we are both scared. I've seen the fear in his face, in his trapped eyes that stare into the distance. In the end, it all comes down to coping with it; getting on with it. It's about breaking free of the undertow and struggling back to the surface. I know now that this is my time. My time has come - to be tough, to take over the reigns, to take things on. It's time to find my skills, my talents; what-ever they are. But we'll do this thing together, as a couple. We are starting to fight back and this time we're a team, a partnership: an unbeatable consortium. So look out life! And don't try messing around with us in future. From now on, me and the other-half, me and my husband, we're going to be fighting these things together - and we'll be punching way above our weight.

There is something I haven't told you about, about the note he left, his speed-written message that stung my eyes as I read. Well, apparently there was no harm intended. It wasn't his idea. His secretary from his old company, the one he took off with, she told him what to write. But I can't say too much about that now. Not now. Not yet. He says that he can't explain why it happened, that he doesn't know why he did it. Freud argued that men have very little knowledge of the real reasons for their actions. I agree - perhaps it's something to do with the seemingly infinite distance from a man's brain to his scrotum. I'm still working on why he did that - my sub-conscious ego may have to re-write that one.

I suppose writing it down did help. Though I realise that our emotions are more complex than words on a page, their illusions created to prevent us from seeing the truth. And the truth is, that love isn't the automatic human condition, being loved isn't a God given right. It's a gift, a reward, an accomplishment. And sometimes that's a hard lesson to learn.

I keep reminding myself of something the poet said to me in the park when I told him my problems that day: he said…'Don't let the past walk beside you. Keep it walking behind; and the further behind the better. If it catches up with you, throw it back over your shoulder like an old scarf.' That sounds like good advice - you can borrow it if you like. Write it down. I've written it on the back of Gerald's harrowing note. Sometimes I touch the poet's encouraging aphorism with my finger; like it's a talisman; like it's a Hobbit message on a ring of gold, saving me from the Swamps of Recrimination, protecting me from an unsalveable resentment. Rejection is hard, forgiving is harder.

# POD

## Stevie Davies

**Stevie Davies's** family came from Morriston but moved to Newton and later Mumbles. For thirteen years she worked as a university lecturer in Manchester. Stevie has published 23 books – fiction, biography, literary criticism and history – and is a Fellow of the Royal Society of Literature. Currently she is Royal Literary Fund Writing Fellow at the University of Wales Swansea. Her last novel, *The Element of Water*, won the Arts Council of Wales Book of the Year award for 2002.

Three kids in four years. I suppose it could be worse: four in three years would be biologically feasible, she's murder, is Mother Nature, considering the diameter of the head to come out and the narrowness of the tunnel to be shoved through, all due to our calamitous bipedal status with no regard for ease of parturition, a design-fault that ...

*Just stop it, Aneurin, stop it now. Put the magazines back. I said ... put them back.*

... is nearly as bloody woeful as situating the vagina next-door to the anus, because next to childbirth cystitis has to be the worst pain, doesn't it, the very worst, I slew in my chair just to think of it and my urinary passage winces, flinches, ouch, as if it remembered, but can tissue actually be said to remember, the delicate, delicate place where such gross pains come to pass and searing pleasures, such violence, such throes ...

*That's right, come and sit here next to Mami, Magdalena, that's right, you snuggle up* ... and the dentally immaculate suited guy reading the Financial Times flashes us a surprising grin, very nice, very sweet, given the trauma we're subjecting him to, and Dr Up-his-own-Arse Williams from the Institute (he doesn't deign to recognise me, I'm just the ex-academic mother of three human nuisances, well stuff you, Williams, stuff you all) reluctantly simpers at Magdalena, and the ginger biddy grins too, and suddenly everyone's smiling, a festival of sunlight breaks in on us, while Magdalena turns and whispers breathily behind her dimply hand,

*Dat man's got hairs up his nose, Mami.*

*Shush Magdalena.*

She's got an unusually carrying whisper. Oh God, Christ, what a darling she is, what a precious beauty, I ache for her, for her father in her, for those wormy little fingers and her mass of brown soft curls against my face and lips. Treorchy-Gran had seven living children, two stillborn, goodness knows how many miscarriages, shucked like a peapod once a year she was, but what's my excuse, educated with the toffs at Cambridge, criminal casualness, I just love fucking, I love it in the way nature intended: pity ratbag nature pays you back with this excess fecundity, this fat billowingness, and there are times I've felt like a pod, a gourd, a clay pot just abjectly mindless brooding on its own rotundity, so damned conspicuous, not human any more ...

*I said, Aneurin, put them down now, stop annoying the people, I won't tell you again.*

Oh what's the use? Marie Stopes might as well not have existed for all the notice I've taken and I *don't* like condoms and I *do* like risks, I expect it's something Freudian, I've impaled and imperilled myself and these little loons are the result. Viola wants feeding, my Christ, does her nappy smell ripe, so, Dr Williams, you're going to get a sight of tittie, that'll put the fear of God in you if the dentist doesn't, watch him vanish up his own arse, old poker-face: remember him chairing the library committee and me wandering in from sunbathing with the third-year students, and I slid in beside him, what was it he said? *At long last we are quorate.* How solemnly he said it, what reproof for female lecturers gassing with a bunch of lads on the grass, sucking from a Coke bottle, in a strappy sun-dress. *At long last we are quorate.* Shuddering with aroused distaste.

And they got rid of me, the wankers. *You have hardly produced at all, Dr Powell.* That's a joke: I'm a one-woman Harvest Festival. *A total of one article in five years shows a certain lack of commitment*, said the Dean. *Well, look on the bright side*, I sealed my fate, *I score with the students.*

Out flops my tittie, pop it in your mouth, Viola, and let sucking commence. She makes such a noise about it too. Little guzzler. All that lip-smacking, slurping, dribbling from the corner of her mouth, her small palm on my breast, Jesus it's still so sensual, the sensations radiating out in a star, ley lines to pleasure, the sweet drag on the womb, I've had many a happy secret orgasm through this, just cross my legs, so, and ...

*That's right, Aneurin, you read the nice article ...*

Aneurin has a premature interest in Things Sexual and Experimental, especially when someone's having a suck, he'll be fingering his willy or, as now, his little blond head (hair wants cutting but I can't be arsed, my God, three scalps, thirty fingernails and eke toenails, the maths of the thing goes into a dimension that's truly round the bend, and that's without adding in the teeth) and you, you snorting, snotty little brat, you're spoiling my fun, you seem to have needles in your gums and want to sink them into my tit when you batten on, mother nature has a lot to answer for.

*How old are the little ones, may I ask?* enquires the foreign guy sitting nearest to our menagerie. Magdalena is standing with one hand lightly on his knee, the other bunched against her lips, just staring. Is she all right in the head, I sometimes wonder?

*Four, three and ten months.*

*Well, really, they are peautiful children.*

*Thank you. I think they're peautiful children too,* I can't resist mimicking. *It's a pain waiting around with them though. I hope we're not disturbing you?*

*Not in the world.*

This I like. *Not in the world.* Meanwhile there's a flurry of coming and going: Old Williams and Ginger have had their jabs and been put out to freeze, and the girl on reception is sneezing away remorselessly over the queue. Give them one, girl, that's the spirit.

*Wot you speak for like dat, Old Man?* Magdalena is enquiring.

*Well, I come from Chermany. In Chermany we speak Cherman. Not Inklish.*

Magdalena is fascinated. Then, without warning or seeking permission, she clambers on to the German knee and gazes into the German eyes.

*Oh glory. Do you mind?*

*I am honoured*, he says. *Let us read a book together, Magdalena.* Off she trots to fetch one. *Such a charming name. Is she musical?*

*Very. On the drum.*

*The drum is a very robust instrument.*

*Especially at five in the morning.*

I swap Viola to the other breast. By God, I'll be a sad, saggy woman after all this suckling which I do *not* do, please note, Eternal Powers, do *not* do to protect my little darlings with my antibodies, no way, though, OK, sure, it makes sense and saves them and me a load of hassle, but because I personally happen to enjoy it, the tender, dragging, horny feeling that puts the light on in your body even when you're overworked, which by Christ you are, you're nine tenths dead by bedtime and feel fifty.

Williams is fingering his jaw in bewildered dismay. Asks Ginger in an undertone how her injection is taking. Blimey Charlie, the old goat, I'm sure he's got the hots for her, shouldn't she be warned about *being at long last quorate*?

He was on that panel that gave me the push. They all fiddled with their ties, while Dean Dai Thomas (whose fingers have been lubriciously active in generations of girls' knickers, pantihose, jeans, right back to corselettes and whalebone bras if the truth were known) enquired was I a mite overburdened? Not wholly suited temperamentally to ...? *No!* I should have said. *No way mister are you taking my livelihood!* But Viola chose that moment to wrench round, grinding her unborn bum on my bladder. My belly stretched so taut I gasped and felt I'd split. Uncharacteristic tears sparked. I fatally crumbled, under bombardment without and battery within. Lumbered up, said, *Sod the lot of you, you dessicated load of coconuts. I resign.*

Pure folly. I heard their basso profundo murmurings behind me. Knew it for a catastrophic mistake the moment I was through the door but at the same time there was an exhilaration, a punching of the air.

I'll reintroduce myself to Colleague Williams. When this little sprog of my loins has sucked me dry - oh for someone to fuck me dry, it's an age since I had a proper shag, by which I mean a shag where you see stars, you can hardly move afterwards and your flesh is so tender and lax that your pee scalds, your legs tremble, oh gorgeous, and the guy is still up for another go - oh for that fuck - anyhow, in the absence (temporary, I trust) of such, when Viola has sucked her fill, I'll introduce myself to old Quorate and watch him squirm. With any luck Viola can do a projectile vomit, I'll aim her at him, she's spectacular at those, I kid you not.

*No, Aneurin, you'll just have to hold on I'm afraid.*

He's whining for a widdle but you can bet, the moment we get into the loo, our names will be called and we'll miss our turn. When I get home I'll dump them for a nap and have a wank. How pathetic is that? Keeps you going, needs must.

*Wow, you are pongy*, I tell Viola. *You are one ripe stinky malodorous lass.* And she suddenly and surprisingly topples her head back like a heavy chrysanthemum and falls fast asleep, dead weight on my left arm. With the burp still in her.

Dr Williams has been called. He looks confounded and doesn't respond. As if by some Kafkaesque turn of events, he found himself transformed into a dental emergency in the middle of a seminar pontificating about his favourite, I don't know, *Welsh adverb*, and suddenly all his stained teeth sprayed out, revelatory, over the somnolent beery students.

*Hi*, I buttonhole him as he picks his way past my bratlings *remember me?* He pretends not to hear my *Hi*, not to see my little Peauties. I should have set them on to him while I had the chance. Why keep a weapon of mass destruction to yourself? But he's gone. So that means we've got to wait for him to be drilled before we get our turn. And all we're in for is examinations.

*Excuse me,* I petition the crazed-looking receptionist. *Can't my kids go in first? Then you'll have a nice quiet place to sneeze and the other patients can rest in peace.*

*Not if 'E says no. What 'E says, goes. Sorry, Mrs Powell.*

*Miss, Ms or Dr,* I say. *Take your pick. But married I ain't. Doesn't matter about the wait. They might as well run riot here as anywhere. Aneurin, come and sit on Ms, Miss or Dr's lap, you yowling little sod.* I yank him by his dungarees.

The guy next to me who's been used and spurned by Magdalena looks at his watch. He read her something about Janet and John, of which she heard not one word, gazing with forensic curiosity into his face, squirming her behind on his knee until she got tired of it and announced her botty was itching. She'd sucked all the juice out of her prey, ground him around a bit on the squeezer and left his skin. If she goes on like that she'll turn into a mantis, either that or she'll have a bun in her oven before she's fifteen. Now they scramble for my lap. It's a conflict Magdalena's bound to win, since I've strapped Viola into the pushchair and Aneurin, for all his cheek, is a coward. When Magdalena comes at him punchy fists flying, with her stocky body, thick little legs and arms, eyes on fire like Boadicea, he has to bow to superior force. I adore her, I adore her. I see Aaron's face in her face swimming up to the surface as the baby plumpness of her cheeks recedes.

*Come here, gorgeous, angelic, peautiful.* I kiss her cheeks and she snares my neck with both arms, lovely and solid, kneeling up on my lap. And she kisses back, with rapture, her mouth open and wet on my cheek. How I cried for Aaron, how I drained my self in tears for Aaron, but ah-ha little did Aaron know, he'd left me with you, my Magdalena.

*I have two children pack in Chermany,* my neighbour confides *Two lovely little kirls. Rosa and Gabi. May I show you a picture?*

*They're dear.*

*Yes, aren't they already?*

He says no more. I ask no more. Funny, pictures of people's children: what can you say? His thin, fastidious fingers restore the two-dimensional girls to his wallet, tucking them into the compartment where they are housed. Nice quiet, paper children who don't require to be fed, potted, washed, hugged, lugged upstairs on your back and lullabyed half the night. Got it easy, haven't you, mister. And what a wallet. Fancy, swanky. Any number of pockets and receptacles. Now that we're on benefit our purse is notably light.

*So you come to us complaining you're skint, are you, having thrown away all your advantages? Don't you know we scrimped for your education, and what have you done with it?*

*Given you grandchildren?*

*Any fool can do that. And Magdalena being, well, coffee-coloured. Aren't you ashamed?*

*Proud,* I said quietly. *Proud. Magdalena is my life.*

*I'd hoped for more sense from an educated woman. But I suppose you're after money, is it?*

I grabbed the cheque, mortified. Done for myself good and proper. Still there was something mysteriously thrilling about being a pod. Going with my tummy spherical, like Plato's all-round men who rolled around without the need of legs, they were so perfect, and the babe-enclosing skin tight as a drum: well, that doesn't sound too pleasant, but ...

*That's the way, Aneurin, you go sleepy-byes, curl up like a kitten ... yes, I know you're hungry, we're all hungry ...*

... but it was a feeling of being ripe, fruity, and lusciously mindless, just drifting on a current, thinking of nothing but the next meal because, talk about hungry, I snaffled Mars bars galore, I was a frigging Mars bar, and I said to Aaron that time, *I'll have your child, Aaron. Then I'll be content. You'll not be able to hurt me, no one will hurt me then, I'll be.*

*Be what?*

*Just be.*

He made no reply but I could see him chewing it over. Well

I got over him. And the others. Problem with kids is, you can't put them away in your wallet until convenient. Because I am ravenous for life. For pleasure. So, Dr Powell, why did you not insure against inconvenience by investing in the pill? Haven't a frigging clue. I seem to have lived in a dream.

Wish I hadn't blown it at the Institute. Good feeling, that was, perched on the desk, swinging my legs in the tiniest skirt and the highest heels whilst confiding the obscene habits of Caligula to an agog packed lecture theatre. Invented novel and ingenious vices on the spur of the moment, on the best scholarly principles. They lapped it up. Gives you a buzz to wow a couple of hundred guys at a sitting. Not wowing anyone much now with my tall tales, my svelte figure. I mean, pods don't, do they? Two a penny in every supermarket. God I could get maudlin if I let myself, I could be hangdog.

Williams reels out. Looks fit to puke. Excellent. So it's our turn? But of course we're all in the land of nod. Some of us are even snoring. We've red cheeks and a sleep-sweat. We're curled up like kittens, we're sucking our thumbs, we're an army that has fallen corporately asleep on the watch. And we are deep asleep, make no bones about that, the waters have closed over our heads and we are full fadom five. Thus it is, Mr Dentist Davies, that you have robbed me of my postprandial wank, which these characters would have granted me by toppling asleep en masse after their beans on toast. Thus it is that your ears will be assailed by god-awful roaring when you wake them up from dreamland. You have buggered up our day, Mr Davies, good and proper, and you will suffer.

Williams totters, a pitiful crock, with flecks of blood on his chin. Obviously one tooth lighter than when he went in. Relief suffuses his face at the sight of Ginger. Salvation is nigh. A female person to moan to, lean on, leech from. And oh is she asking for it. *Leech me! Leech me!* You daft bugger.

*Mrs Powell, would you all like to come through?*
*Ms, Miss or Dr.*

*Oh, yes, right, Mrs Powell.*

*I'm not married, you see. Powell is my name. I'm not Mrs.*

*Well, anyhow, would you like to come through?*

*Oh yes, that will be very easy, won't it, now that they're all fast asleep.*

*Well, I'm sorry, Mrs Powell, we've been running late as you know, what with sickness and understaffing, we do our best.*

*I'm - not - Mrs.*

*Tell you what, if I take the little one, you could carry the little boy and … we could come back for …*

*Allow me,* says the Teutonic white knight. *Allow me to transport my, if I may so style her, little friend Magdalena.*

So my trinity of young souls trumpet-voluntaries its outraged dolour, its berserk triumph over the forces of fogeyness, bellowing fit to wake the dead, which, as Mr Davies jests, is handy, since it serves to pop open everyone's mouth for inspection, without need of coaxing or bribery, and all at once we are out in the street and headed for home, fish fingers and an hour's serious solace under the duvet.

# MYSTERIOUS WAYS

## Belinda Bauer

**Belinda Bauer** trained and worked as a journalist in Cardiff, before going to California to study screenwriting. She has now returned to live in Cardiff, where she writes films for a living. 'Mysterious Ways' is her first attempt at a short story, so she was delighted to have success with it. She plans to write more fiction in the future.

There's a missionary sparkle in the eyes of the man sitting next to me and there's only one thing worse than flying, and that's flying with a zealot. And a fat zealot, with arms like legs, spilling over the armrests and obscuring my attendant call-button, so that by the time we're halfway across the Pacific, I need several drinks, more dry-roasted peanuts, and a tranquiliser dart to fell the half-man half-hippo half-in my lap. None of which I can call the attendant to bring to me.

He's taking bibles to Bora Bora. I wonder where they got a dog collar big enough to go around his neck. It's like a cummerbund. The people of Bora Bora need bibles, apparently. They're wonderful, simple people, but they do need bibles. Many, many bibles. I wonder how many bibles I could stuff into his big sanctimonious mouth at one time.

The movie is Braveheart, which he talks through - quietly but zealously.

A big bang

Did they have guns in those days?

*

There's salt and grit in my mouth and my neck is burning, but my legs and belly are cold cold cold. Why am I lying down? And where's my attendant call-button? At least the missionary has shut up.

A few seconds after I open my eyes, I realise I am on a beach. It's not difficult - white sand, green sea, palms swaying. For miles. Alone. I am very alone.

Apparently the plane simply fell out of the sky, but I can't remember it, to my relief.

I'm hungry and there are several crates and boxes washed up further down the beach, so I get up slowly to have a look. Belatedly, I check that neither of my legs has been torn off by a shark. I read about a surfer who lost a leg to a shark and didn't even know it until he tried to wade out of the water and toppled over. I'm on an even keel though.

The nearest crate is further away than it looks. Like Alpha Centauri. It takes me two hundred and thirty seven paces to reach it. Somehow that seems significant, although it turns out later not to be. Each pace scuffs up the perfectly smooth sand. As I get closer to the crate I start to worry about how I'm going to open it. It's very big - about four feet high and eight long – and looks sturdily made. But when I reach it I can see that two planks have been splintered at one end, and it doesn't take much tugging to pull one off completely.

The crate is full of Bora Boran bibles as – deep in my heart – I knew it would be.

*

I walk to a rocky outcrop at the end of the beach, and there are eleven crates, each stuffed full of bibles. Black, laminated in plastic, and indigestible. I clamber onto the rocks, and look across to another long, long stretch of sand, identical to my beach, but without crates.

I calculate just how many bibles I am sharing this place with and, based on an estimate of the size of each book, and struggling to remember basic geometry, come up with about 2,500 per crate, which makes a total of 27,500 bibles, each weighing - well, not much, but altogether? No wonder the goddamned plane crashed.

I see yet another crate below me, wedged between two rocks and half-in the water. There seems to be something dark waving beneath it. I move around the rocks, trying to get a better look, but even though the water's crystal clear, the size of the crate and the shadow it casts makes it hard to see. I scan the sea. No large predators evident, so I slide into the water.

The salt stings my eyes at first and makes them hot and blinky, then I focus on the missionary, who's bumping gently under the crate, with his fat fingers stuck between two broken planks, and who - even though his eyes are open - is quite dead.

I scrabble backwards and shoot out of the sea and sit shaking on the rocks.

I wonder how long he clung to the crate before a wave turned it over. When he discovered, too late, that his fingers had swelled, and that all the time he'd spent praying he should have spent practising holding his breath in case of just such an emergency. Like me. I can hold my breath for two minutes and thirteen seconds.

Anyway, that takes the total to 30,000 bibles.

\*

The foliage around the beach is impenetrable and I can't find any of the exotic fruits which are supposed to be on desert islands. The last thing I ate was breakfast on the plane yesterday, which was an omelette, which I didn't eat because it had mushrooms in it, and a croissant which I didn't eat because they're just pure fat. So the last thing I actually ate was supper on the plane the night before, which was a very small piece of steak surrounded by green stuff, which I don't eat, so I just had the steak, three marble-sized potatoes, and half a canned pear with so-called chocolate sauce on it. I'm also really thirsty. And hot.

\*

There's dew on the leaves the next morning, although it takes me a long time to lick enough leaves to make the thirst subside. I rip the laminated plastic covers off several bibles and furl them into cones, then half-bury them in a hole covered by palm fronds, where the dew should fall. I cut my thumb ripping off the covers and some of the fake gold stuff which spells out Holy Bible gets in the cut. The word of God has entered me. I'll probably die of blood poisoning.

Even though I'm not as hungry as I was yesterday, I know I will be again. There are coconuts on the trees, but they are forty feet above my head. Fish is the obvious choice. I reckon the dead missionary must be attracting a lot of nibblers, so that's where I start.

The tide is out, so I build a wall of bibles near to the waterline at the rocks. It's about eight feet long, two feet wide, four feet high, and curves like a crescent moon with its points facing the shore. It takes me ages, although I don't realise this until I'm standing in three feet of water.

The next morning there are three small cups of water under the palms, and two small fish in my trap. I know I can't be starving, because the thought of eating them disgusts me, so I scrape the salt off some of the drying bibles, smear it over the fish, and drape them over a crate to cure, or whatever the hell fish do when you leave them in the sun.

Disappear, in this case, as a gull swallows both of them. I make a wild swing at the gull and shock both of us by grabbing one yellow leg. It turns itself into a mad, flapping, squawking cartoon-gull in my hand and, more to shut it up than anything, I flail at it with a bible, which breaks its neck. I make a bad job of plucking it, and decide to joint it using one of those sharp plastic bible covers. The insides aren't in little plastic bags like they are with chickens. I wish I'd never started, and retch twice.

I collect lots of dry wood and ball up pages from the drier bibles for kindling. I rub two sticks together for the rest of the day.

*

Three fish this morning, and they must be a different kind, because they don't look as unappetising as the others. Also some kelp. Tastes like tyres, so I just pop the bubbles, which reminds me of Christmas.

Before it gets too hot, I use a couple of hundred bibles to spell out big letters HELP in the sand. Maybe God will see it, ha-ha.

I build a drying rack for the fish, with a clever laminated-plastic roof, which lets in the sunlight, but not the gulls. As the sun gets higher, I notice that the light falling through the plastic is concentrated in places into intense pinpricks. I hold a page from Job under the plastic until it starts to smoke. I cook the gull.

*

I build the hut after the first rain. A bible on your head offers little protection against a tropical storm, I have found. The hut starts out as a crude windbreak, but ends up a black laminated igloo. It sucks up heat during the day, and dispenses it graciously at night when I crawl inside.

I dive under Missionary Rock to find said missionary missing part of a thigh, but otherwise reasonably intact. I wonder if he cursed God. I take his dog collar and make very viable sunglasses by poking two tiny holes in the fabric and tying it around my head over my eyes.

Fishing is good. I catch a small shark one day, but am too nervous to kill it. I tell myself I am letting it go because I admire its perfect grace.

I scour the horizon and the sky for rescue. Perhaps no one around here speaks English. I spend the day changing HELP to SOS.

*

I have a loose tooth, which makes me think of Mutiny on the Bounty. Why can't I discover any breadfruit on this godforsaken place? I try again to find a way through the jungle, but am scratched and scared of losing my way or of stepping on a snake. Maybe it's loose through natural causes.

*

My tooth falls out. I cry like a little baby. I want my mum. I would suck my thumb, but I'm scared of dislodging more. Obviously they were right about fruit and vegetables.

*

It takes me a long time. The bibles are good bricks, and I take care to align them as accurately as possible so that a small error down here at the base will not be magnified a thousandfold at the top.

They are hot to the touch and the plastic covers are almost tacky, so they are pretty firm once they're in place.

I use the trunk of the smallest tree as the central stanchion for my spiral staircase. It takes me a lot longer than I think it's going to. Twice it collapses as I test it, and I have to make it even wider at the bottom.

On the seventh day I touch the coconuts.

I go carefully downstairs for my last armful of bibles to make sure I'm balanced, then I dislodge a nut by hitting it repeatedly with a plank. I tug it off the stem and hold its green coolness against my chest.

As I turn to go downstairs, I stop for a moment to look at my beach.

My hut looks very small from up here. I notice one of the S's in SOS is rather out of shape. The white sand bordered by the green jungle and the jade sea is beautiful. It looks different from up here. It looks like Paradise.

I drop the coconut and, miraculously, it splits open on the sand. I hurry down the stairs and break off a piece of the flesh. The flavour fills my whole body, it is so delicious. I break off a bigger piece and walk over to the wonky S. I start to pick up the bibles to move them into line properly, but almost before I know it, I've dismantled most of the first S. I go on to pick up the O and then the other S too.

I pack the bibles carefully back into a crate.

Maybe one day I'll find another use for them.

# PATCHWORK

## Ruth Joseph

**Ruth Joseph** was always a frustrated writer of fiction, during which time she wrote for many women's magazines, had a series with BBC Wales, when she 'cooked on the radio', and later published a cookery book, *The Complete Dieter*, in 1984. Now an M.Phil Creative Writing student of Glamorgan University, her short stories have been published in Bima magazine and several are awaiting publication in *New Welsh Review* and *Cambrensis*.

They have confined me to a hospital bed. They think I am ill. But they are wrong. I am happy, content within my cell-like withdrawal. The alabaster whiteness of the walls and the bleached linen of the sheets have created a perfect cocoon. There is no sink, no toilet. Nothing where I can eliminate, evacuate. But I have my ways. The nurse in charge of me is not vigilant. She uses my toilet time to phone her friends. So far I have been lucky.

Every day a doctor comes to visit me. Although he's a he, he is not a man. He just wears man's clothes and a starched ivory coat – a bloodless arrangement of person with a stethoscope around an anaemic neck and pewter grey hair. He is accompanied by a nurse, brings a weighing scales and talks to me of food, of eating, of gaining weight, of the outside world, of my need to join these people. But I have no such desires.

Some days a window cleaner washes the outside contaminated glass of my window. He is man. I watch him as I lie in my bed. I see the tight t-shirt pulled over muscled shoulders; the arms etched with dark hairs, ligaments roped like strong twine, pushing a chamois over the glass. He pretends that he does not see me. He is told to keep his eyes averted.

I have brought my patchwork. It projects my mind away from their constant nagging and uses up a few calories. I was going to cut the pieces here. I would enjoy watching the silver steel of my tailor's knife lacerate and cleave seams carefully sewn. But they found the scissors concealed in my bag and removed them. I suppose they thought I might do something with the blade. Close with a suicide's bracelet? They do not understand.

I was allowed to bring the pieces ready cut. My mother supervised the preparation. She said that it would not be good, not be perfect, for all the fabrics are different and for a patchwork quilt each fabric has to be of equal density and of similar type. But flawlessness is not the object of the making. She always needs the ideal, always striving for the unattainable that I, too am supposed to crave. I like to mix the colours palette bright in my colourless cell, lying on my blanched bedcovers. They vibrate with their own violent energies.

I start with my brown cotton striped school dress. They do not understand the pleasure I derive slicing and bruising the fabric. There is a smell about it – a damp, sweaty chalky mix of cooked cabbage and fecund bodies. The carved wooden panels ache with the fears of the inadequate. Ink-splotched desks hold their young captives prisoner. 'We expect you to do well. We did not have all your advantages. Your mother and I were lucky to get out when the rest of the family perished. We have had to work, save, and sacrifice for you to get to that school.'

Cut it with knives. Blade its existence. Sew it into something that is mine. My design – perfectly imperfect.

Royal Blue is the uniform towel from my school showers – a nauseous smell of chlorine, foot dip and cheap deodorants. 'Please Miss. I can't do games this week. Can I be excused? Can I be excused showers?' The cream and dark green tiled walls shiver with the echoes of the misunderstood. I have developed early. I am a full-breasted woman with a mid-European bone structure, solid, heavy. My nipples are tight, erect with fear. Lithesome girls with tight, tiny breasts nudge each other, giggle behind my back. Some are staring. I run my fingers over the harsh terry cloth. 'It will spoil the patchwork,' my mother says. But it has to be executed. Cut it. Make it into pieces. It has lost its life.

Yellow is the seersucker tablecloth from my home. It lay on the kitchen table listening to the murmuring of the ancient fridge and the constant bubbling of a pot on the stove. Sometimes it is chicken soup, steaming with golden carrots, onions, and celery, creamy barley and beans, or green pea soup so thick we would joke about having a slice for supper. My mother's tiny green glass vase from her first life sat on that cloth. It had been wrapped in a peasant shawl with her candlesticks and a few photographs when she ran. I'm sorry I broke it. Yellow is the cadmium colour of the wallpaper of my bedroom, of golden egg yolks and rich butter, of sticky dried apricots chopped with peel and moist bananas crushed with the zesty juices and rinds of sharp, knobbly lemons. Whip them together. Beat in the sugar. Fold in the soft white flour. Make a cake for Daddy for his tea. Not for me.

Pink is the nylon tulle dress from my Barbie. 'Why do you have to have such a doll? We never had such dolls in the old country. Such a strange birthday present for a child of thirteen!' But she is perfect. She is beautiful. She is thin with long, blond silky hair, shapely breasts, no stomach and no sex hair. I want to be her. She makes it impossible. Cut her dress. Finish it.

Purple is the colour of my cheap lycra bathing costume. We sit together – a day at the seaside. But the parents keep their clothes on. My father rolls up his black trouser legs exposing white skin and blue, cabled veins. My mother unbuttons her blouse a little. I see creases in her breasts. She looks at my father. They laugh and then a little uncomfortable, they look at me. My mother's face goes pink. I do not like the feeling. I do not like the look my Uncle Saul gives me when I have to relinquish my towel from around my body, to run into the sea. Though when I am away from them, it is beautiful. I taste the smack of the wind hitting my face, the fingers of the warm sun, touching, loving, unconditional. But then I have to return. To Uncle Saul's eyes smirring over my body, through the stretchy costume to my secret places. Cut into slivers with the honed silver steel. It curls as it cuts. Decimate its existence.

Mamma does not fuss as we slice my old pinafore into neat squares. The background is cream with tiny green and pink flowers. Though she does not see why it has to go. It saves the good clothes…always save…keep for best. Help Mamma in the kitchen. We have to cook a special meal. Uncle Saul is coming for supper. Mamma is excited. Gefilte fish to start – fluffy, poached balls of fish lying cold on glass plates decorated with a slice of carrot. Then borscht, soup the colour of blood… 'Grate the beetroot darling. Uncle Saul loves a good soup.' Then Mamma takes the boiling chicken that has flavoured the soup and sets it in a casserole to brown with rice in its bed and more carrots. Dessert is my job. 'Make the pastry. You have such a light hand.' I enjoy rubbing the sticky margarine into the flour with a little vanilla sugar, and seeing the whole come to a pliant ball with lemon and egg. Mamma has gone upstairs to wash and change. Uncle Saul comes early. I have just finished putting the sliced apples into the pie with cinnamon and sultanas. I am putting the pastry on the top. I used to love the smell of cinnamon. Now I hate it. Cut up the apron. Get rid of its face.

Red is the colour of my best Shabbat dress, now a year old. I love its sleek velvet fabric and the garnet colour is reminiscent of autumn light through the synagogue stained glass windows. It is Friday night – the highlight of the week. We sit around the solid dining room table laid with the best snowy, damask cloth. The polished silver candlesticks bear ivory candles; they cast a gentle flickering luminance over the waiting family. The kiddush cups have been polished bright and two vast crusty challot sit under their white embroidered cover waiting for my father's blessing. He trickles the blood-coloured liquid into the silver bechas. It is one of my favourite sounds. We stand for kiddush – the Sabbath blessing. As we rise, the white pearly buttons on my dress pop, exposing my new bra. My little brother giggles and my father mutters something to my mother about me developing and having a suitable dress for a woman, not a child. But I do not want…

Grey is the colour of my father's face. I have no fabric for his face. I hear him talking to the doctor outside my door – hushed sounds not words.

My mother is upset that I want to cut all these materials. 'It is a waste to cut up good things. They could be passed on and I could sell the red dress,' she says. But the doctor is on my side and says they have to indulge me. When he visited me this time, he wanted to examine my body. As he pulled back my nightdress, revealing my shrunken breasts and bloated stomach, he discovered the belt from my red dress pulled tight about my waist. 'What is this here for?' he said gently, as if talking to a small child. 'It keeps me safe,' I whispered. I dare not tell him that every day I pull it a bit tighter. It stops my appetite. 'But it is stopping your blood,' he said in his sing-song voice. Yes, my blood has stopped, the other blood, the woman's blood. When the doctor goes, his face too is grey like my father's. I pull off my nightdress and look at my body. There is no mirror in my room. It is not allowed. They say that I am thin – that I could lose my life, but I only see fat, bulges of blubber poured into skin, covered by a soft fluffy down.

My father returns. He has talked to the doctor. He says that if I would eat a little, I can go on a long holiday to Italy. Sit in the sun. Drink coffee in a dusty piazza. Lie in a chair watching mists clear over slate-blue mountains with tall cypresses standing on tiptoe for a better view, listen to cicadas sounding like old wristwatches being rewound, and gentle bird song in vast magnolia trees.

I am going to try to eat. My father's grey face upsets me too much. I do not want to hurt him.

**

I am sitting at the side of a glittering lake. Small ochre and terracotta-coloured buildings cleave to gentle slopes and the sounds of clinking church bells bless the sunlit landscape. The colours of my patchwork have found new meaning.

The brown and white striped cotton has been pin-tucked

and transformed into an arch of reeds at the edge of the lake safe-keeping grebes, mallards and a flotilla of swans. Beneath, below its ankles, rainbows of small fish arrow through craggy shards of granite and marble.

Blue is the lake water – navy and turquoise wrinkled silk sprinkled with sequins of sunlight basted to a muslin sky and pinned and tacked by tiny pen-and-ink sailing boats.

Yellow are the fields of sunflowers, rough cloth of girasole that point their seeded heads to the warming sun, and fields of maize, their spires golden as they ripen and climb to the light.

Pink is the polished marble of Verona. We feel its hardness and its history at our feet as we walk. Pink is also the colour of soft tulle sunsets on the lake when the sun is tired and waits for the silver attendance of the moon.

Purple is embroidered bougainvillea, hugging sunlit loggias with violet passion. And freckles of tiny scabious and wild cyclamen decorating, petit point, the hedgerows and cool, shady woods where blackberries and blueberries wait for the plucking.

My apron is now a sunlit meadow of light cotton organza which holds its summer flowers outstretched to the light. It is the host to ancient olive trees spreading convoluted branches, legend telling as they sit and wait for another harvest.

My colour red is still wine, but not the bloody, fortified stuff of religion. It is the light pourings of crushed grapes tasting of warm vineyards and laughter. Red is also the colour of my new cotton sundress. My mother is pleased. She tells me it is a good shape and that I look better.

My father has lost the grey from his face. He makes jokes with my mother and from time to time I see him look at me. They think that I am cured and this makes them happy.

Except Italy has given me a new way of living. I have discovered a way to eat which keeps them and me contented. They see me eat pasta with rich tomato sauces. Relish pizzas crisp out of fire baked ovens, lick ice creams made of crushed strawberries folded with whipped cream, feast on peaches and nectarines from gentle orchards with the bloom kissing their skins.

But now I have discovered a trick. It is a conspiracy between my two fingers, the back of my throat and my stomach. I eat my whole meal. They watch and smile at each other. At the end of the meal, I make myself excused and then it is done – a couple of minutes and all is eliminated. It is easy to check that everything is out. At last, I can taste and eat all the things I would never allow myself. Sometimes I eat just for the eating. I force down cold pasta waiting for tomorrow's sauces, ice cream and chocolate till my body will burst with the forcing. In the black velvet when they are asleep with only the rhythm of the fridge playing its music, I stuff...gorge... lust after food. But my woman's blood has not, will not, return.

**

We are home. Italy is past. Smudgy grey skies saturated with ice skewers of rain make stabbing autumn sounds on the outside of the house. They talk of my education. I must go back to school. I do not want to be with those people. Tomorrow Uncle Saul and Aunty Millie will eat with us. He is here now, staying the night as he wants to go to our synagogue tomorrow morning with my father. We have been busy all day preparing a special meal for Rosh Hashono – the Jewish New Year. In the fridge are two fat balls of pastry, resting, waiting for me to attend to them. The one pastry is a light short crust that I have to make into a pie: the other is richer for biscuits.

All last night, I lay on my bed immobile, rigid with fear. It is now early morning and I cannot stay in my room. I need to eat to drown the furies. But I have to be careful now I am home. They watch me all the time. The doctor has warned them. He is suspicious about my condition – my little conjuring trick. As I walk down the stairs I feel my heart banging in my throat. My body shakes. My stomach is screaming. I go to the fridge door. What can I take? There is a whole chicken, intact – I can't touch that. We have made knaidlech – small dumplings to boil in the soup. I push them in my mouth, raw salty dough, putting others together so that they will not detect any disappearances. I go to the cupboards. Cereal, raw cereal without milk, dry so that it makes me cough: fingers in golden syrup, strings sticky over my body. Faster, faster, two lumps of pastry. I cut pieces and force it in without tasting. My heart beats so fast. I feel dizzy and faint. I sink to the floor. The black and white ceramic tiles are cool to my throbbing, bloated, overheated body. I look across at the dog's bowl. My mother has put the spare pieces of meat from the soup flavouring. The dog has had enough. I look around. My father will be down soon. The day is about to start. The pieces of meat in the dog's bowl lie calling me. I take the bowl and force greasy pieces of meat into my mouth.

There is a sound at the door and Uncle Saul walks into the kitchen wearing an old faded silk dressing gown. I see his face drawn with horror.

# The Rhys Davies Short Story Competition

In 1990 Lewis Davies, the last surviving sibling of Rhys Davies (1901-1978), made the financial gift which established the Rhys Davies Trust. Under the chairmanship of first Dr R. Brinley Jones and later Professor Dai Smith, and with Professor Meic Stephens at the helm as secretary, the Trust set forth to both foster Welsh writing in English and to perpetuate the memory of Wales's greatest short story writer.

A chosen device, which would not only encourage the production of new work but also keep alive the spirit of Rhys Davies's short fiction, was the open literary contest. The writers of Wales were encouraged to compete for a substantial money prize, attention, kudos, publicity and publication. The Rhys Davies Short Story Competition, run every two years by the Academi with the financial support of the Trust, has become a feature of the creative writing landscape. The opportunities the Competition offers attract hundreds of entries each time – new and established authors mix anonymously. Their output is judged not by their names but by the quality of their work. As a by-product Rhys Davies, Welsh fictioneer of an earlier age, is rediscovered by a new generation who may otherwise never have found the opportunity or the reason to read his work.

There have been four competitions to date, judged by some of Wales' most accomplished writers. In 1993 Leonora Britto won with *Dat's Love*, which became the title story in her first collection of stories. In 1995 the prize was shared between Rachel Palmer's *The Sleeepwalker and the Glazier* and Nigel Jarrett's *Mrs Kuroda on Pen-y-Fan*. (Published in *Tilting at Windmills*.) In 1998 Lewis Davies won with *Mr Roopratna's Chocolate*. (The title story in the 1998 anthology of the winners.) This present anthology represents the winners of the 2001 competition. The winning story was *A Sort of Homecoming* by Tristan Hughes.

**Rhys Davies** (1901-1978) was one of the most prolific and unusual writers to emerge from the Welsh industrial valleys in the twentieth century. Born in Blaenclydach, a tributary valley of the Rhondda arising from Tonypandy, he was the fourth child of a small grocer and an uncertificated schoolteacher. He spurned conventional education and left the valley, which was to be the basis of much of his work, at the age of nineteen, settling in London, which was to remain his base for the rest of his life.

Early in his literary career, he travelled to the south of France where he was befriended by D.H.Lawrence, who remained an influence in his writing. Though sex remained, for Davies, the primary determinant of human relations, he differed radically from Lawrence in that he saw the struggle for power rather than love, either sexual or emotional, as the crucial factor.

Though the bulk of his work was in the novel he achieved his greatest distinction in the field of the short story. Having few predecessors, Welsh or English, he drew his inspiration and models from European masters: Chekhov, Maupassant, Tolstoy and Flaubert. His view of humanity was classical in that he saw people as being identically motivated whether in Biblical Israel, Ancient Greece or the Rhondda Valley. Much of his output was concerned with women, who almost invariably emerge triumphant from any conflict.

He was a gay man at a time when it was difficult to live openly with his sexuality. He lived alone for most of his life and avoided relationships which seemed to betoken commitment on his part. His closest friendships were with women. He avoided literary coteries and groups, and held no discernible religious or political convictions. He lived, to an intense degree, for his art, which, such was his reticence, has received public attention only in recent years.

He was awarded an OBE for services to Literature in 1968.

# Academi

The Academi is the Welsh National Literature Promotion Agency and Society of Writers. It works through the medium of both Welsh and English. It was founded in 1959 by Bobi Jones and Waldo Williams. The Academi promotes literary events throughout Wales, runs the popular Writers on Tour scheme, organises literary festivals, book launches, conferences, tours and other events. It works on behalf of writers and readers, fiction writers and poets, litterateurs and storytellers. It is associated with the publication of three magazines: *A470*, a what's on guide to literary Wales; *Taliesin*, Wales' leading literary journal in Welsh; and *The New Welsh Review*, Wales' leading literary journal in English. It originated the *Oxford Companion to the Literature of Wales* (editor Meic Stephens), *The Welsh Academi English-Welsh Dictionary* and is currently working on *The Academi Encyclopaedia of Wales* to be published by University of Wales Press and Harper Collins in the autumn of 2004.

You can join the Academi as an Associate for as little as £15 (waged) / £7.50 (unwaged). Associates receive *A470* to their door, are entitled to priority and discounted entrance to Academi literary events and also enjoy a range of further benefits including discounted book purchases at Waterstones and some other bookstores. Applications should be sent to Academi at 3rd floor, Mount Stuart House, Mount Stuart Square, Cardiff CF10 5FQ.

Further information is available at www.academi.org

The Academi and the Rhys Davies Trust are planning a fifth Rhys Davies Short Story Competition. Short fiction will be sought on the theme of Cardiff and urban living. 2005 is the centenary of Cardiff as a city and 50 years of Cardiff as Capital of Wales. Further information on the competition can be obtained by sending a stamped addressed envelope to the Academi at P O Box 438, Cardiff CF19 5YA; by e-mailing rhysdavies@academi.org or checking our web site at www.academi.org

New Welsh Short Fiction from PARTHIAN

# Mama's Baby (Papa's Maybe)

'The biggest anthology of Welsh fiction... a major achievement.'
*The Western Mail*
£7-99 ISBN 1-902638-03-4

# A White Afternoon

'Betrayal, bisexuality, strippers... seriously good.'
*The Western Mail*
£6-99 ISBN 1-902638-00-X

# Tilting at Windmills

'Fine writing and thought provoking scenes. Welsh writing may well be a growth industry.'
*The Daily Post*
£4-99 ISBN 0-9521558-18

# A Human Condition
# Rhys Davies

This selection of fiction marks the centenary of Rhys Davies' birth and includes some of his best work.

Dark, witty, and acutely observed, these finely-crafted stories put small-town life under the microscope. In his unique and memorable style, Davies examines the strange games that people play. He paints vivid portraits of the human condition.

'A Welsh Chekhov'
*Sunday Times*

'Rhys Davies is a first-class writer and every short story... a novel in itself.' John Betjeman, *The Daily Telegraph*

'Gently wrapped, these stylish perceptive tales have centres as hard as steel, and are all the better for it.' *The Guardian*

'Rhys Davies's characters all walk straight out of the page and hold one with an almost physical attraction.' *The Times*

Rhys Davies grew up in the Rhondda. A prolific writer, he produced novels, plays, essays and an auto-biography, but it is through his work in the short story that he forged an outstanding reputation as a writer of skill and originality.

ISBN 1-902638-18-2 £5.99

**www.parthianbooks.co.uk**